DAMAGE

AN ARRANGED MARRIAGE MAFIA ROMANCE

NATASHA KNIGHT

ABOUT THIS BOOK

We're a match made in hell, Stefan and I.

He took me to exact his revenge. I went from being a pawn to my father to being a pawn to Stefan. The only difference is I have a ring the size of a boulder on my finger and a husband I don't want.

And the hardest part is I thought he was different. I thought I was falling in love.

I guess my father was right. I'm not a very smart girl.

Stefan is a powerful man. He doesn't play nice, not if you're his enemy. But I've learned one thing about my husband.

He takes care of what's his.
And I am his.

His enemies have become my enemies, but he'll never let anyone hurt me. He's fiercely protective.

It's the predator inside that scares me.

***

*Damage is the second book in the Collateral Damage Duet.
If you have not yet read Collateral, you need to do that first. You
can pick up Collateral in all stores.*

PROLOGUE

Gabriela

Waves swell in the wake of the speedboat, lifting me up then dragging me under while gunshots fire around me. Someone shouts an order but I'm under again, swallowing water, choking on it.

"Are you going to drown me too?"

Instinct takes over and I kick.

Arms paddling wildly, I manage to break the surface, gasping as I suck air into my lungs.

Waves again, and gunshots. A flurry of them.

I think that scream is mine.

In the dark, I see our boat bobbing and swim to it. See one of the two men slumped over the side as the other frantically reloads his weapon.

It's no use though. They have machine guns. A pistol doesn't stand a chance against a machine gun.

More shouts and I'm picked up by a wave again and

when it drops me down, my elbow slams against hard wood, the pain electric.

I push through it to grab onto the side of the boat and hold tight, but the reprieve is only momentary because the bigger boat speeds closer and I wonder if they're going to crash right into us. If that's their intention.

I don't have to wait long to find out because the man on our boat stands. It rocks violently and when he dives over the side, our boat capsizes. I lose my grip and scream, my head crashing against the hard wood and what was once my salvation becomes my undoing as I go under.

Under.

"Are you going to drown me too?"

I asked Stefan that question.

The waves don't carry me up as I go limp and I watch the sliver of light. A floodlight, maybe? I watch our capsized boat go down. Watch the man who'd been slumped over the side float away, blood from his wound turning the water crimson when that light momentarily shines down on him.

I don't know if my eyes close or if it's that dark. How can it be so dark? I'm floating, my arms rising above me as I become weightless.

The sound water makes when you're immersed, it's almost other-worldly. The gurgling, bubbling, as the shock of cold, of dark, take me deeper.

Water through my hair. Water through my fingers. It feels like an oily, slippery eel.

I watch myself as if I'm out of my body. As if it's not real. It can't be.

I'm drowning. Like her. Like she drowned.

Like she *was* drowned.

I have to wake up.

I have to swim.

Panic.

Salt burns my eyes, but I turn my face up toward that light. I kick and push against the water and there's someone else. Someone in the water. It's not the dead man. He's long gone. Down in that dark. Food for the fish.

My lungs burn. I'll never make it.

But then there's an arm around my middle and it's strong. Stronger than me.

He's a powerful swimmer because we're moving, rocketing up.

I gasp when we break the surface.

A hand in my hair pulls painfully and I remember that day. I remember the lake. It was a black night like this one, the sliver of moon offering only the barest light.

I remember my mom. I see her now.

I see her that night. Wet and cold and terrified, her hands bound behind her back as he dunked her again and again and again and she gasped and choked, and I watched. I just watched.

I feel pain as that grip tightens and I'm under again and I fight. I fight like she couldn't, and someone laughs when I break the surface only long enough to suck in a single, gasping, wet breath before I'm down again, underwater, the sea gurgling in my ears, a hand keeping me down.

Nothing peaceful about this drowning. I wonder if it could be peaceful, after the pain. After the terror. I don't think so.

No salt in the lake. That was a blessing. Did it burn as much when she sucked water into her lungs?

"Enough!" a man shouts in Italian. "He doesn't want her dead for fuck's sake. Haul her up."

Pain again because he's pulling me up by my hair. A

moment later, I hit a hard surface. I turn onto my side and cough up water and vomit, half-choking on it.

Men talk. Someone yells. The engine rumbles beneath me and we're moving.

Someone strikes a match and a moment later, I smell a cigarette. Small details. Why am I concerned with small details?

"She done puking?" someone asks.

A nudge at my hip, my back.

I roll my head and my eyes burn when I open them to see the dark form looming over me, faceless and menacing.

"She's awake."

"Then get the hood on her, idiot!"

The faceless man grunts and leans down. For an instant, I see his yellowed teeth as he laughs, sticks his cigarette between his lips. Ash falls on my face and when I feel the hood being drawn over my head, I fight. I don't know how, but I fight, screaming, clawing at arms, a face, a wet eye.

"Fucking cunt!"

The kick comes hard and fast, knocking the wind out of me. I curl into myself, hugging my middle. I think for all my father did to me, he never beat me. Not like this. His punishments were calculated. Thought out. Strategically placed.

"Fucking scratched my fucking eye!"

Another kick, this one to the back of my head and maybe I'm grateful for it. Grateful that I don't have to think about the smell of the sack over my head. Grateful that I pass out as I'm lifted, my head lolling painfully over the careless arm—not like how Stefan carried me. Not at all.

And maybe I'm a coward, but I'm grateful to black out.

1

STEFAN

"Find her!"

I slam the phone down, spin on my heel and run my hand through my hair.

Two days. It's been two fucking days and no word. Not a single goddamned, mother-fucking word.

"Fuck!"

Soldiers rush in and out, Millie trying for the hundredth time to get me to eat. I'm not fucking hungry. I want her back. I want her back now.

My cell phone rings. It's still in my hand and I look at the screen.

Marchese.

Fucking Marchese. Finally.

I answer.

"If you send any more of your men to any of my properties, I'm going to offer a fucking bonus to anyone who kills one," he threatens.

"I will search every one of your properties until I find her."

"Where the fuck is she? What the fuck did you do to her?" he barks.

"She'd be here if you hadn't sent your men to fucking pick her up! We had an agreement."

"When my daughter calls me in the middle of the night begging me to help her get away from you, you can bet your ass I'm going to send my men. What did you do to her? Did you hurt her? If you hurt her—"

"If your idiots hurt her—"

"Fuck!"

I suck in a breath. I fired every man on the roof that night. Because how did an inexperienced, unarmed girl—a fucking girl—get down to the cove and into a boat without them seeing?

Marchese called me at six that morning asking where his daughter was and when I told him what had happened —still not quite convinced it wasn't his men on the bigger boat—he sounded panic-stricken.

But I'm more likely to believe he's a good actor.

"If I find out you have her, Marchese—"

"I'm not scared of you, Sabbioni. You'd know if I had her."

I exhale. As much as I hate having to work with my enemy, I can't believe he wants his daughter hurt. Or worse. "We've searched the island. She's not on it."

"She's not in Rome."

"Someone knew she'd be out there. This was planned."

"How would they know?"

"I don't fucking know. That's my question too and since you're the only one she talked to before leaving, you can see why I have fucking questions. Now for the last fucking time, did you stage the kidnapping?"

"Get your head out of your—"

I disconnect the call. He's not going to tell me anything new.

She must have taken her phone with her and I'm guessing it's at the bottom of the sea now because the tracking device comes up empty. She fell in. I saw that. Saw it in the floodlights of the speedboat, an unmarked and unnamed boat, too far for me to see anyone's face.

They pulled her out, though. They must have. I have to believe that.

If they went to that much trouble to get her, they don't want her dead.

But I should have had a call by now. If it's money they wanted, I should have had a call.

The door flies open, and I spin around to find Rafa rushing in.

"I have a lead!"

"What lead?"

"I think they took her to Pentedattilo."

It takes me a moment to register the name. To place the location. "In Calabria?"

Rafa nods.

"It's a fucking ghost town. Are you sure?"

"I'm not sure but it's the first clue we have. I've sent men from Taormina. It'll be faster for them to get there."

I stop. "Your father's men?" Francesco Catalano is my uncle. His wife, my aunt, was my mother's sister.

"*Your uncle's* men," Rafa states. "I figured this was more important than your feud."

I grit my teeth.

"Get the jet ready."

"Being fueled as we speak. Let's go."

I nod, stopping in the study to pick up my revolver and tucking it into its shoulder holster.

"Where's your weapon?" I ask Rafa.

"In the car. I'll drive. I'm faster than your guys."

"Take this," I tell him, tossing him a pistol. "I'll drive."

We step outside where Rafa's SUV is waiting. I notice the deep, long dent on the passenger side, the white paint marring the shiny black of the SUV.

"You think you're in any condition to drive?" Rafa asks as I bypass his SUV and climb into the driver's side of the Bugatti.

"My car is faster." I tip my head toward his, noticing a similar dent and scrapes of paint on the driver's side. "And judging from the damage on your vehicle, I'd say I'm the best choice. Are you coming or not?"

His brows furrow together but he climbs into the passenger seat and not a moment later, tires scrape gravel, sending up a dust storm as I speed to the gates, exit the property and make it to the small airstrip where my jet is housed in just under fifteen minutes.

The captain and small crew await, and we board. They must know this impromptu trip is not a social one. No one talks or even greets me apart from a nod from the captain as Rafa and I board. A few moments later, we're in the air.

"What was your tip?" I finally ask.

"My father has friends in the area. Two nights ago, there was talk at a bar about a girl. One of his informants followed the men and noted unusual activity."

"And he just decided to tell us now even though I'm guessing he knew of Gabriela's disappearance two nights ago?"

"He wanted to be sure, Stefan."

I'm not sure I believe it, but I know Rafa. His relationship with my uncle, Francesco, is not an easy one. And it drives me insane that he still seeks the old man's approval.

"What was the unusual activity?"

"Two vans. Blacked out windows. Looked like they carried a bundle inside and they've had the building guarded ever since."

"A bundle." Christ. I suck in a tight breath.

"She'll be okay, Stefan. If they wanted her dead, they wouldn't have gone through the trouble they did."

I nod.

It's less than an hour before we're climbing back out of the plane at Calabria's regional airport where Rafa has arranged a car for us. Well, his father has.

I try to shove all thoughts of my uncle out of my mind. I need to focus.

Rafa and I ride in the same vehicle. It's just over an hour as we approach Pentedattilo. I haven't been here in over twenty years but seeing the cliff town brings back memories.

My mother had a special fondness for places like this. Abandoned. Old. So much in Italy is old I'm not sure why it fascinated her to the degree it did. Pentedattilo is a ghost town now, with few inhabitants. But the tourists still come piling in.

"Get around them," I snap, sliding my window down to yell at them to get the fuck out of the way.

The driver honks his horn, and someone gives us the finger. I'm tempted to shoot it off.

Rafa puts a hand on my shoulder. "She'll be okay, Stef. We're almost there."

I turn to look at him, see he's got his phone out. He's tracking the locations of the men his father sent.

I try to relax, forcing myself to breathe a deep breath in.

The tourists thin out as we climb deeper into the town. I'm grateful for the stifling heat keeping the throngs away.

The four SUVs behind us follow along.

"How many men does my uncle have up there?" I ask, trying to decide if it's better to go on foot.

"A dozen sharpshooters." He turns his phone toward me, and I see the red dots situated in buildings surrounding the one we suspect Gabriela is in.

"How many are guarding the property?"

"Three outside. There are six total from what they saw."

I wonder if they thought we wouldn't find the place or if they wanted us to find it when I hear that number.

"Keep driving or go on foot?" the driver asks me when we're about two streets away.

I rub my jaw, the back of my neck. This is easier than it should be, which makes me question why. "Only six men?"

Rafa nods. "You want them to take out the guards outside?"

I shake my head. "No kill shots but incapacitate them if we need to. None of them will walk away anyway, but I have questions. Let them know we're coming by cavalcade."

He nods and sends the message to the soldiers surrounding the property as well as those in our vehicles . He waits to receive confirmation.

Once we have it, I gesture to the driver, taking my pistol out of its holster as we drive on.

I see the first two men when we turn the corner. They look almost weepy from the heat. They're leaning against the wall of the building, each smoking a cigarette, each with a machine gun slung over his shoulder.

"Where's the third?" Rafa asks.

I'm already scanning. "There. Taking a piss." The man is the first to see us as he walks out of the bushes along the side of the road. A look of panic crosses his features and I watch as he fumbles with one hand on the fly of his jeans while trying to get his gun with the other.

Before he can get either done, he's down.

The shooter must have a silencer on his weapon because although I don't hear the shot, I know exactly when he hits his target in the right knee, dropping him instantly as he screams in agony.

"So much for a quiet entrance," Rafa says.

"My entrance wasn't intended to be quiet," I say, opening the door as the SUV comes to a stop. I see another of the soldiers drop as a third raises his arms high in surrender.

Francesco Catalano's men step out of their hiding places and Rafa flanks me as we walk toward the entrance.

"Stefan, you should wait until we have the soldiers contained."

"I'm not afraid of these men. They have what's mine."

A machine gun unloads and we take cover as the shooter appears in the upstairs window. Bullets spray the SUVs. A moment later, the shooting becomes erratic as he's hit by one of our men and his body flops over the windowsill, the glass of the window long gone.

The machine gun finally drops to the ground and the shooting ceases.

The door bursts open and a soldier rushes us, weapon ready. Another man appears at a different window upstairs.

They get a couple of rounds off before I hit one and one of our soldiers takes out another.

At my signal, the men spread out around the building.

"On your knees. Hands behind your head," I yell to the one guard who surrendered like a pussy when we pulled up.

He obeys instantly, but his gun is still strapped to his shoulder.

I take it, sling it over mine. I lean down, grab him by his dusty hair and make him look at me.

"Any more men inside?"

"No!" he shakes his head frantically, looking at the dead one in the window.

"And the girl?"

He's shaking, blubbering.

"The girl," I ask, fisting his hair hard.

"Out back."

I haul him to his feet. "Take me to her." I shove him ahead of me into the building.

It's dark, the only light streaming in from the few glass-less windows. The interior is completely destroyed, the stairs half-ruined. Any furniture that's still recognizable is rotting and the place stinks of piss and earth.

Better than the morgue, I tell myself.

I push him along. The house is deeper than it appears from the outside.

Rafa is behind me along with two other men. Our weapons are drawn, in case anyone lied and there are more armed men inside.

We walk through two more rooms, stepping over debris, the bones of some unidentifiable animal.

"If you're fucking with me," I start.

He shakes his head, moves through an opening that was once a door to a walled-in courtyard. The walls are high and in the center is a well and I'm going to fucking kill him when he goes directly to it. He shoves the piece of wood covering it aside.

I hear her before I see her. Her gasp echoes as sunlight pours into the deep well.

I look down.

Something moves and she screams, pulling her knees in and the terror in her voice makes every muscle in my body tighten.

"Gabriela," I yell down, shoving the man aside and

leaning the machine gun I took off of him against the well. A soldier takes hold of him and I peer down. The well has got to be sixteen, maybe eighteen feet deep.

Rafa is beside me in an instant. He looks down at her.

"Fuck," he mutters.

She's huddled against a corner on her knees. Her hands are bound behind her and a hood covers her face. Something runs across her lap, a mouse maybe, and she screams again.

"I'm coming, Gabriela. I'm coming to get you."

I don't know if she hears but she's trying to stand, to press her back into the wall.

"Here," Rafa says and I look at him, at the rope ladder he's unraveling into the well.

"We're throwing a ladder down. Just be still, Gabriela. It's me. It's Stefan. I'm coming."

I climb down into the cold, damp space. The rope is old, and I have to be careful.

When I get closer, she starts screaming again.

"It's Stefan," I tell her, taking hold of her shoulders, pulling her into me. Holding her tight.

The instant she knows it's me, her body goes limp and she begins to sob, her hooded face buried against my chest.

I look around. I'm glad the well is at least dry. They didn't have her sitting in filthy water.

I pull back to look at her. She's covered in dirt and shivering and for as hot as it is up there, it's fucking cold down here. Although I think without that covering at the top of the well, it would have been worse for her.

She's cold, but she's alive.

I have to hold her upright as I look around the small space, see the hole the mouse must have disappeared into, see the carcasses of bigger animals rotting nearby.

It's probably better she had that hood over her head.

"Stefan?" she manages.

I hug her again, hear her whimpering softly beneath the hood.

"Are you hurt?"

She makes a sound and leans against me, her face, her torso, her weight fully into me. I want nothing more than to pull that hood off. To look into her eyes. To see for myself she's not hurt. To tell her she's safe.

But I need to get her out of here before I do that. She'll panic if she sees what's down here.

The rope ladder concerns me, though. She's too weak to climb on her own but I'm not sure it will hold both of us.

First, I untie the rope at her wrists, rub them, eyeing the bruised, raw flesh, the marks on her through the ripped tatters of her clothes.

Her hands move to the hood, but I capture her wrists.

"Let me get you out of here first," I say.

"I want it off."

"Trust me, Gabriela."

She hesitates, then nods. "Okay," comes her small, trembling voice.

"We're going to climb up," I tell her, trying to keep my voice calm. I have to carry her up. I have no choice.

When I pull away, she cries out. "Don't leave me!"

"Shh. It's all right. I'm here. I'm not going anywhere."

"Stefan," Rafa's voice calls down when he realizes what I'm going to do. "The rope isn't strong enough."

"It has to be," I say. I turn to Gabriela who can't see me. "Wrap your legs around me," I tell her, lifting her up.

She barely manages and I wonder if they've given her food or water in the last few days.

"Good. Now hold on tight and don't let go no matter

what," I say, folding her arms around my neck and holding her to me with one arm wrapped around her.

I keep her like this for a moment before beginning the careful climb up. My progress is slow and the rope strains beneath our combined weight. When I'm about two-thirds of the way up, it tears beneath my foot and Gabriela screams, clinging so tight she's almost choking me.

I stop moving. Hug her tight to me.

"It's okay. We're okay."

I look down. I look up.

"A little farther and I can take her," Rafa calls to me.

I move again, carefully but as quickly as I can, hearing the tattered rope strain with every move, and just as Rafa takes hold of Gabriela, the rung I've got my feet on rips away, the ladder dropping to the well floor, leaving me dangling.

She screams again, but Rafa hauls her up and I shift my grip to the edge of the well and hoist myself up and over.

I go to her, ignoring the burn of the rope on the palms of my hands. I take hold of her shoulders, pull her to me once more before taking the hood off. Relief floods through me at seeing her bruised, tear-stained face again.

She blinks, squints. It was black where she was, and the sunshine is bright.

I move her into the shade of the house. After a few moments, her eyes adjust and when they focus and she sees me, she breaks down into a sob and cleaves to me and I think how scared she must have been. How terrified.

And I know I'm going to kill these men. I'm going to kill them slowly.

"I want the men lined up outside. On their knees," I tell Rafa, cupping the back of her head, keeping her close.

"On it."

Without a word, I lift Gabriela in my arms and carry her out. One of our men opens the back door of the first SUV and I set her inside it.

"I need water," I tell him.

He nods, goes to the trunk and returns with a bottle. I take it from him, open it. I haven't taken my eyes off her once as I brush matted, dirty hair back from her face. I hold the bottle to her lips, and she takes a sip.

"Make sure none of those tourists get close," I tell the soldier. "Station men on either side of the street."

"Yes, sir."

I pet the tangle of her hair, look at the dark spot on her temple. Notice the old one on her forehead and remember the damage to Rafa's car.

But that's a question for another time.

With my thumb, I wipe away a tear. I rub her skull, feeling for bumps, but I don't find any. I note each bruise on her neck.

Where her top is ripped, I see the bruise on her side, and another near her belly button. I can make out the print of a shoe and rage boils inside me.

I touch each mark softly, making a mental note, shifting my gaze to her thighs, to the marks there, and down to her feet. She's wearing one running shoe. The other foot is bare.

I meet her gaze again, tilt her face to mine. "Did they touch you?" I force myself to ask and I can see the effort it takes for her to shake her head.

Her gaze widens when it moves over my shoulder and I know the men are ready.

She pulls me to her when I draw back.

"I want to go. I want to get away from here," she manages.

I nod. "We will. I need to take care of this first. Do you

know which ones put the bruises on you?" The others will have a swifter death.

She glances over my shoulder and I follow her gaze when it focuses on one man in particular.

"Him?"

Before she looks back at me, I see her exchange a look with Rafa.

My muscles tense and my eyes narrow when I look back at my cousin and he quickly shifts his gaze.

"I don't know," Gabriela says. "When I woke up, I was in a van and they never took the hood off."

"Did they give you any food? Water?"

"Water once."

"Okay. You'll wait down the hill for me."

She shakes her head, wraps her hands desperately around my shoulders. She opens her mouth to protest.

"Shh," I say, again cupping her face. I kiss the first tear that falls, taste the salt of it. Then kiss her forehead. "I don't want you to see this."

"I don't want to be alone."

"You'll do as you're told now. The driver and another soldier will be with you. You're safe. I'll be there in a few minutes."

She looks over at the kneeling men again. At the dead one still flopped out of the upstairs window. He got off easy.

"You're going to hurt them?" she finally asks.

"Yeah. I am. For every mark on you, they'll have twice that from me." *Before I throw them into that well to rot.*

I leave that part out.

She studies me, those sad sea-foam eyes understanding I won't let this go. Is that because she's a Marchese? Would someone outside of our world understand?

"Okay," she says.

I nod, but before I let her go, I need to say one more thing. "I didn't hurt Alex, Gabriela. What happened to him, it wasn't me. I swear it."

She freezes and it's like she just remembered. A moment later, her face crumples. I take her in my arms, and she sobs again, silent sobs that wrack her shoulders. I hold her, cup the back of her head. Feel her like this, feel her giving herself to me in her grief.

"Go on now, let's get this done and go home, okay?" I whisper in her ear.

I feel her nod as I draw back. The driver and another of our men get into the car after I give them instructions and once the SUV is out of sight, I turn to the kneeling men awaiting their sentence.

2

GABRIELA

I shiver in the backseat of the SUV as we wait for Stefan and the others. We're parked just outside of the town and tourists pass by on foot, laughing with each other, waving fans to cool themselves in the stifling heat, children playing as they run up ahead of their parents.

And all I can do is sit here and think about what's happening up there. What Stefan is doing.

How was this going on just blocks from where I was trapped?

The driver looks at me. "Too cold?"

I drop my arms, shake my head no, even though I am.

I think about Stefan, how he came for me even though I was the one who ran away. How he risked himself to carry me out of that well. I have no doubt he didn't remove the hood because what I would have seen down there would have terrified me.

I think about how gentle he was. Like the other night when I'd cut myself breaking his bottle of whiskey. Gentle and caring. Like I mattered. Like he actually cared about me being hurt.

My mind wanders back up the hill again. He's not being gentle now of that I have no doubt.

If I strain to hear, is that a bullet being fired or is it my imagination? Will Stefan really kill all those men?

Don't I know the answer even as I ask the question?

I am a Marchese, after all. My father may not appear to be as brutal as Stefan, but I know him. I've seen first-hand what crossing my father can do.

My thoughts move to Alex and the thought of his death, of his vicious murder, makes my stomach hurt. He didn't deserve to die. And he didn't deserve to die like that.

How am I going to tell Gabe? How will I explain it?

And do I believe Stefan?

I remember Alex's text and realize that my iPod is gone. It's at the bottom of the ocean with the dead man.

I'll never be able to go back and reread old texts, revisit old stories. The fact that I'll never see him again hits then. Even though I know he's dead, it's like I'm only now realizing what that means.

I will never see Alex again.

I will never talk to him again. Never hear his voice.

If it wasn't Stefan, *if* I believe him, then who?

But why would Stefan do it? What would he have to gain? Especially after talking to him, he knew Alex was no threat, not in any way. In fact, if he does care about me even a little bit, he'd know that it would hurt me to hurt Alex.

Is that why whoever did it, did it?

Guilt knots my stomach but I'm distracted by the cavalcade of black SUVs with their dark tinted windows coming our way.

I see Rafa first. He's driving the first SUV and Stefan is talking to him. Rafa looks at me. His expression doesn't change when he does.

The man up there, the one I recognized, I think he was the one driving the car that rammed into us the other day. I'm very sure, actually. I couldn't forget those eyes if I tried.

So, was it the same person who ordered the chase that ordered my kidnapping? And how did the kidnappers even find me when they did? The only person who knew where I was was my dad and he wouldn't have done something like this.

Would he?

The procession comes to a stop and Stefan climbs out of the front seat, leaving Rafa alone in the vehicle. He gets into the back seat with me.

He looks at me and I at him and I see how his hair is a little mussed, see how he's absently rubbing the knuckles of one hand with the other. I almost expect to find a splattering of blood on him, but I don't. Although he's dressed in black from head to toe so maybe it's just that I can't see it.

Our driver takes the lead and the other SUVs follow ours.

I realize I never buckled my seatbelt when Stefan leans over me to buckle it.

"Are you okay?" he asks.

I nod. "What did you do to them?"

He studies me. "You don't need to be a part of that."

"I already am, aren't I?"

"You recognized one of the men."

I swallow, take a sip from my bottle of water.

"We'll talk about it later," he says. "At home."

Home.

"The phone you gave me, it's gone," I tell him. "I lost it in the water. I'm sorry."

"That doesn't matter, Gabriela. What matters is that you're safe."

"Who took me?"

"That's what I'd like to know." He holds out his phone. "Call your father."

I look at it, but I shake my head. I have too many questions I know my father won't answer. Like how he knew so quickly what had happened to Alex. Like how there was a second boat out there. How it came right toward us like those men knew exactly where we were.

Stefan types out a text. "I'll let him know you're safe."

"Stefan?"

He hits send and looks at me, tucking his phone into his pocket.

"Did my father do this?"

I can see from the look on his face he's considered this.

"I called him twenty minutes before I went outside. How did that other boat get out there so fast? How did they know we'd be out there at all?"

"That's what I'm going to find out."

I look out the window. Could my father have done this to me? Is he that wicked?

"Where are we?"

"We're in Calabria. It's on the mainland and the town they held you in is called Pentedattilo. We'll take the jet back to Palermo. Or we can get a hotel room, get you cleaned up, get some food if you want."

I shake my head. "I want to go home."

There's that word again.

Home.

Do I even have a home?

He reaches over, takes my hand, squeezes it. "You're safe now. Nothing's going to happen to you ever again. I swear it."

3

STEFAN

Nothing's going to happen to you ever again.
I swore it.

But can I guarantee that? Obviously not.

I look at her while she stares straight ahead. I think she's still in shock. And part of me, it's pissed at her. Pissed at her for walking out of the house and onto that stupid boat. For putting herself in this situation.

And the other part wants to hold her close and never let her go because when I saw her at the bottom of that well, hell, before that, there were moments when I thought she might be gone.

There were moments these last couple of days where I thought she'd drowned.

Fuck.

I tug at my hair.

What the fuck is wrong with me?

I killed every one of those men. I did it slow. Bullet after bullet placed to inflict pain but not kill. Then I dropped them into the well. Some survived the drop. I heard them down there. And I walked away.

I'm a monster, I know that. What would she think if she knew exactly what I did? Would she run from me?

As if I'd let her go.

I laugh out loud and see how her gaze snaps to me.

She doesn't talk much during the trip back home, but I'm surprised when, as soon as we're back and she sees Millie, she goes straight to her and lets Millie envelope her in her arms, breaking into sobs the moment she's there.

This is a girl who grew up without a mother. A girl who grew up without affection. Physical touch. At least not the right kind.

Millie hugs her hard and I see the look of concern on her face. She was worried about Gabriela. This arranged—no, let's be real here—this *forced* marriage, I don't know what I expect from it. I haven't thought it through on any level, actually. Other than I am taking her from Marchese, I haven't given thought to what I'd do with her. To how real this marriage will be. I haven't considered what her days will be like.

I haven't cared.

And it's not that I care now, I tell myself as Millie looks Gabriela over and tells her she'll make her something to eat and get her something to tea.

"I want to shower. And throw these clothes away," Gabriela says.

"Millie," I start, not looking at Gabriela. Not sure I can without taking her in my arms and I'm not sure if it's to hug her tight or to shake her so fucking hard, I may do more damage than those men did. "Did you get in touch with the doctor?"

"Yes. He's on his way. He should be here any minute."

"Good." I run a hand through my hair, not quite able to

focus on anything but this chaos of emotions inside. "Take care of it. I'll be back."

I walk away. I don't say goodbye to Gabriela. Don't say a word to her. I just walk out of the house and I can feel Gabriela's unbelieving eyes burn into my back.

But fuck her.

She brought this on herself. I haven't lied to her once and when I told her about Alex, she didn't believe me. She called her fucking father to be rescued from me.

The urge to throttle her has my hands fisting as I step into the Bugatti and drive into Palermo. I go straight to Rafa's house. Just walk right in and make my way to the living room, pouring myself a whiskey before I sit down.

When he sees me, he seems surprised. He's on the phone. I notice his hair's wet and he's changed his clothes. Mine still have crusted blood on them.

"Stefan," he starts, disconnecting his call. "Something happen?"

I swallow my drink. "Yeah, something happened. I think you were there for it."

He gives me a strange look, opens his mouth to say something but I shake my head.

"I'm pissed, Rafa."

He turns to walk behind the bar and get a glass.

"I'm fucking pissed. She could have been killed and my men didn't even see her go. Fucking idiots."

He walks to the couch, carrying the bottle of whiskey with him.

"You fired them. The new men will know better to look out for her." He pours himself a whiskey and refreshes mine.

"Seeing her in that well..." I give a shake of my head. "It fucked with me. I don't care about this girl. I hate her, in fact. I should, at least." I finish my drink, rub the back of my neck as Rafa refills my glass once more.

"But you don't. You like her."

I turn to him. "I don't fucking *like* her. I'm not fucking sixteen."

He makes a face like yeah right.

"What happened to your car?" I ask, abruptly changing the subject.

"Nothing," he says, casually turning his gaze away. "Sideswiped someone. Probably shouldn't have been driving."

"Sideswiped two cars at once?"

"Wall on one side."

"When?"

"Couple nights ago. Doesn't matter."

I study him. Remember there was paint on both sides of the car. But I decide to drop it. "I'm grateful to your father," I say, swallowing the bitter taste the words leave.

"He'll be glad to hear it. But you should tell him yourself."

I nod my head, finish my drink and stand. "Let's go out."

———

IT'S LATE WHEN I GET BACK TO THE HOUSE. I PASS GABRIELA'S room when I get upstairs, only pausing for a second. Once inside my own room, I hit my shin against the baseboard of the bed as I stumble to take off my shoes and socks.

The balcony doors are open and it's a stormy night. I walk outside.

I love rain in Sicily. It's so rare and when it comes at night, fuck, it's something to see. I stand there in it, stand there getting soaked.

I look at her doors. The curtains billow in the wind and

rain blows inside. She should close them. I walk to her room wondering how she can sleep with all this noise, momentarily panicked that she snuck away again.

But she's here. She's in her bed and asleep under the covers. Out cold. I wonder if she slept at all during her captivity.

I brush hair back from her face, take in the bruises. She looks peaceful. And even with the bruises, she's still beautiful.

It could have been worse. They could have really hurt her, but they didn't.

This wasn't about hurting her, though. Someone's sending a message.

They can take what's mine.

My hands fist, fingernails digging into my palms. I will kill whoever did this. I will demolish them.

I pull the blanket back, stumbling a little when I do. I'm drunk. I should go back to my room. But I don't want to.

Gabriela stirs, but doesn't wake.

She's just wearing a pair of powder blue cotton panties. No top. I can see why. She's got bandages all over her, a large one wrapped around her lower ribs. Did they break her ribs?

A gust of wind blows so hard that it knocks a vase over, sending it crashing to the floor.

Gabriela bolts upright, startled awake. I don't know if she processes where she is. When she sees me, she opens her mouth to scream. I don't think she realizes it's me. It's dark enough she wouldn't see my face.

Without a thought, I'm on the bed, my hand over her mouth pushing her into the pillow.

"Don't," I tell her.

She struggles, her broken nails sharp against my skin.

"Stop. It's me. Gabriela, it's me. It's Stefan."

She blinks as a cloud clears the moon and, in the light, she sees my face. She stops fighting and I move my hand from her mouth. She pulls up to a half-seated position.

"Stefan?"

I look at her, at her naked breasts, small and pretty, her nipples hard. My mouth is watering to lick that tight little tip, take it into my mouth and suck, just a little, just enough to make her moan.

"What are you doing in here?"

I don't answer. What am I doing in here? Didn't I come in to close the balcony doors?

She looks over at the clock and so do I. It's a little after two in the morning.

I shift my gaze to her breasts again. I reach out and touch one nipple with the back of my hand, just brushing my knuckles over it. It hardens and when I shift my gaze to hers, I see how her cheeks flush, how her throat works when she swallows.

I want her.

Even now, like this, I want to have her.

I lower my gaze to the bandage.

"Your ribs," I say, touching the gauze.

"Bruised. That's all."

"That's all?"

"Stefan," she starts, pulling the covers up to cover her breasts. "Are you drunk?"

I grin, take hold of the blanket and tug it out of her hands.

"Not drunk enough," I say, moving to straddle her, my knees on either side of her hips as she lays back and I cage her in with my hands to the sides of her face. "I didn't know," I start, leaning close to her, inhaling her clean scent.

"I didn't know if they pulled you out of the water." Her hands come to my shoulders. "I didn't know if you were alive or dead."

"I—"

"I didn't fucking know, Gabriela."

I lay some of my weight on her, careful of her ribs when I see her wince. Sliding one hand behind her head, I weave my fingers into her hair and tug her head back to tilt her face upward.

I look at her like this. At her parted lips, her pretty eyes. That bruise on her forehead that was there before everything. "Why did you look at Rafa when I asked you about that man?" I ask. I don't know why I ask it.

"What?"

"When the assholes were lined up and I asked you who hurt you. You looked at one man in particular then at Rafa."

She lowers her lashes, looking fucking guilty as sin.

I squeeze my hand in her hair and she winces.

"Stop, you're hurting me," she says.

"Why?"

"Stefan, stop it."

I smile down at her and something akin to jealousy burns in my gut.

"Were you with him? When his car got sideswiped?"

She tries to shake her head and when she answers no, she shifts her gaze away and I know she's lying. I know she's fucking lying.

I loosen my grip on her hair, grit my teeth.

"Why are you wet?" she asks, brushing my wet hair back from my forehead.

That touch distracts me. It's soft. Tender.

"What?" I ask.

"You're soaked," she says.

I look down at myself then back at her. "Rain." I lean in close to her, brush my jaw against her cheek so my mouth is at her ear. "You're not off the hook with me, Gabriela."

When I draw back, I see that same caution I've seen before. Not fear like what I saw when I took that filthy hood off her head, but she is wary of me.

"What do you mean?" she asks.

"I mean you ran away. You snuck out of the house and in doing so, you almost got yourself killed and you did get yourself hurt. You'll answer for that."

She doesn't reply. I'm not sure I expect her to.

"You're in no shape to do so now, though," I say finally, standing. I need to go. To get out of here. Because if I get into bed with her, I will want things.

I straighten, look down at her. I run a hand through my hair.

"Doctor's coming tomorrow," I say.

"He just came today."

"He's coming again."

"Why?"

"Birth control."

Her mouth falls open. Not what she was expecting, I guess.

"We're moving the wedding up."

"What?"

I lean down so my face is inches from hers. "You better not lie to me again, Gabriela."

She stares at me.

I turn and walk back out onto the balcony, into the rain. One of the metal chairs screeches when I stumble into it before making it into my bedroom and collapsing on my bed.

4

GABRIELA

I don't sleep after that. I can't.

We're moving the wedding up? Why? What does my getting kidnapped have to do with the wedding?

Is it because he wants to fuck me? Is he so honorable that he won't do it before the wedding?

Even as I think it, that word, honorable, makes me sneer. Because what if I say no? What then? How honorable will he be then?

There are two sides to Stefan Sabbioni. Maybe more than two. One is violent, filled with rage. The other is the one who carried me out of that well. The one who swore he'd never let anyone hurt me again.

I don't know if I can reconcile the two.

When the doctor comes the next day, he gives me the birth control shot. After he leaves, the seamstress is back with the final fitting of the hideous wedding dress. Millie's in and out too and there seem to be double the guards as there were before.

The only person not here is Stefan.

I'm surprised when Millie walks into my bedroom that

afternoon to tell me my father is on the line. She's holding a house phone out for me. I guess I don't expect him to call me here.

"Dad?"

"Gabriela. Why haven't you called me?" Not *are you okay*?

"I'm just trying to wrap my brain around it all myself."

"Well, I'd have preferred to hear from you that you're all right rather than that man."

"*That man* saved me."

"He should have had you better protected. I'll kill him if anyone touches a hair on your head again."

How heartfelt, I think, rolling my eyes. "Well, I'm on the mend if you're concerned."

Silence. "Of course I'm concerned," he says a few moments later. "Don't be stupid."

"The men on the boat, are they both..."

"Gone. Yes."

"I'm sorry about that."

"It's their job. They knew the risks."

Still. It's two lives. Two more lives gone because of me. "He's moving the wedding up," I tell my father. He sighs and I realize something. "You already know, don't you?"

"Yes."

"Doesn't what happened change things?"

"Why would it?"

"Because I nearly died."

He makes a sound like a snort or a chuckle. "Don't be dramatic, Gabriela."

I'm shocked. But why am I shocked? I know my father, don't I?

"Did you arrange it?" The words are out before I can

stop them and the instant they are, I swear I feel ice on the line.

"Did I arrange for men to kidnap my daughter and drop her into a well?"

It's his tone that has me quieting. That has me remembering those moments in the water when I'd thought of her. My mom. His tone and the silence after that remind me of that night so many years ago and even though we're separated by hundreds of miles, even though I can put the phone down and just walk away, I shudder, freeze up.

My father still scares me.

And I'm very aware that he's not denying that he had anything to do with it.

"Waverly is sending over a revised contract. Be sure to read the modification before you sign it. I'm sure as heroic as you must think your husband-to-be, he won't have shared this little tidbit."

"What modification?"

"It'll be hand delivered. I have to go, Gabriela."

"What modification?" I press.

"Goodbye."

I hear a click and he's gone. For a moment, I stand listening to the dial tone before finally putting the phone down.

I sit on the edge of the bed and run my fingers through my wet hair. I touch the bruise on my forehead, the one from when Rafa and I were driving, and those men side-swiped us. It's the same person who arranged for me to be kidnapped because the man Stefan was asking about was at both events.

Why didn't I tell him that? Tell him about Rafa and Taormina and that man?

There's a knock on my door and Miss Millie comes inside with a tray of food.

"Shall I take this?" she asks about the phone once she sets the tray down. She doesn't ask me how the call was. She knows better. Or maybe she just reads it on my face.

"Yes, thank you." She's about to leave when I stop her. "If he calls again, can you tell him I'm not here please?"

She studies me for a moment, then nods her head. "Of course, dear."

On the second evening, I go downstairs for dinner because if I spend one more minute in this bed, I'm going to go crazy. There's a replacement cell phone on the table at my place with a note from Stefan stuck to the box.

Don't drop this one at the bottom of the sea.
S

The joke is in poor taste, but I find myself smiling anyway.

I take it out of the box. It's the same pretty rose gold as the original phone and the same numbers are programmed.

I check the time. It's almost noon on the East Coast. I program the number for Clear Meadows and ask the receptionist for Melanie. She connects me a few minutes later and I ask if it's a good time to FaceTime Gabe. I can hear the smile in her voice and a few moments later, using Melanie's cell phone, I'm looking at Gabe sitting in the community room with a smock on that has paint smeared all over it.

"Gabi!" he calls out and I see his finger coming toward the camera. I guess he's trying to touch my face.

"Gabe! It's so good to see you!"

"What happened to your face?" he asks.

I touch my bangs, push them down to cover the bandage.

"Oh, it's nothing. Just fell down. You know how clumsy I am."

"You're not clumsy." He peers closer, the camera showing me just part of his eye and nose for a moment. "You're hurt," he says, his expression so worried, it breaks my heart.

"I'm okay, Gabe. I promise. It's just a little bump."

He just sits there studying me for a moment and his expression is almost like it used to be. Like *he* used to be.

But then it's as though he suddenly remembers something and shifts the phone to his knee where there's a scrape covered by a band-aid.

"I fell too, Gabi. We have matching band-aids."

I smile when I see his face again. "How did you fall?"

"I tripped when I was running."

Melanie comes into the picture. "We had a rainy day and the minute we could get outside Gabe went charging, didn't you, Gabe?"

"Yep," Gabe says. "But it doesn't hurt. Are you coming for lunch, Gabi?"

"Not today, Gabe, but soon, okay? I promise."

"Tomorrow?"

Crap. "Not tomorrow, no, but soon. It'll be a surprise!"

"You used to come visit me more."

"Gabe, why don't you show Gabi your painting?" Melanie asks, saving the day because Gabe gets a proud smile on his face and a moment later, I'm looking at a large canvas of mostly smeared paint in all different colors.

"It's modern," Gabe says.

"It's beautiful," I say. I think about what Alex said in his last message about wondering if he'll ever be able to talk to

Gabe without breaking down afterwards. I wonder the same thing.

"This one is for Alex," he says, as if reading my mind. "But I'll make you one next."

How am I going to tell him that Alex is gone?

"I can't wait to see mine!" I say, my enthusiasm overdone.

We talk for another five minutes, but I can see Gabe getting distracted as he picks up his paint brush again and, after a promise to FaceTime him again the following day, we disconnect the call.

Miss Millie must have been waiting for me to wrap up because no sooner have I put the phone down then she's outside serving dinner. Tonight, there is a whole roasted chicken with potatoes and green beans.

"This smells wonderful," I say, inhaling. "But it's a lot of food just for me. Is Stefan going to be home for dinner?"

Home. The word weirdly sounds more and more normal.

"He'll be here later tonight, after dinner. You just eat what you like."

"You know you don't have to wait on me," I tell her.

"I like it, Gabriela. It's my pleasure. I'm just happy you're home safe and sound. Now go on and eat. Let me know if you need anything and make sure you save room for dessert. I made you something special."

My smile is authentic. "I will, thanks, Miss Millie."

I eat on my own. I eat more than I think I will but that's probably because the last few days, I've been eating so little.

When I'm finished, I go into the library, take a book off one of the shelves and curl up on one of the armchairs.

I'm so absorbed in the story that I only realize three hours have passed when I hear footsteps approaching and sit up, closing the book.

It's Stefan.

The library door opens, and he stands in the doorway.

My heart thuds against my chest as I look at him. He's wearing a black V-neck T-shirt and jeans. His thick hair is perfectly in place, and the dark shadow on his jaw accentuates the sharp line of it.

I look at his big hand on the doorknob and see that ring and I think about what he's done with those hands. The violence he did to those men. The gentleness with which he held me.

My gaze lifts to his forearms, the muscle beneath the dusting of dark hair. Something stirs inside me. Inside my belly. It's like a fluttering of butterfly wings.

I'm attracted to him. In spite of it all, or maybe because of it all, I'm attracted to him.

He saved my life.

But it could have been him to set me up, couldn't it? Why would I rule him out? He's the one who gave me the phone. Maybe it was like I thought. Maybe it was bugged.

I shake off the thought. I don't believe that. I just don't. Maybe it was the look on his face when he took that wretched, vomit-stinking hood off me. Maybe it was the fact he climbed that ladder down and wouldn't let me go as he carried us both back up, even as the rope tore. I don't know, and although I'm sure he's no saint, I don't believe Stefan would do that to me.

When I draw my gaze back to his, I find him watching me.

I think about how he was when he came to get me. When he brought me up out of the well on that ladder. When he held my hand and swore he'd never let anyone hurt me again.

When he came into my room drunk later that same night and warned me my reckoning was coming.

The look in his hazel eyes tells me tonight is that reckoning.

"Gabriela," he says, coming into the library and closing the door behind him. Locking it.

Why do I note that one act?

He walks toward me and perches on the ottoman before my chair.

I sit up and put my hands on my knees. "Stefan," I say, because he's not the only one who feels justified to a reckoning.

"Doctor says you're doing better, healing nicely." He looks me over. When he reaches out to touch me, I pull back, making him pause for a moment before his hand is on my middle, my ribs.

He's feeling for the bandage.

"It's gone," I say.

"Good."

"Where have you been?" Thoughts of Clara cloud the edges of my mind, but I force them away.

"I spent a few days with my uncle in Taormina. He's the one who told me where you were."

"What?"

"Rafa's father, Francesco Catalano. Our relationship is... difficult, but I owed him a debt of gratitude."

"Rafa's father?" Was he the man Rafa met with when we were out there? Why didn't he tell me?

"Yes."

"How did *he* know?"

"Someone overheard something probably from the men on the boat bragging about what they'd done."

"I don't understand."

He studies me, stands up and walks across the room to look out the window into the dark night. "You don't understand because people are duplicitous." He turns back to me and when he approaches, I see his gaze momentarily drop to the photo album on the side table beside my seat before shifting back to me. "Only a fine line delineates between an ally and an enemy, and that line is constantly shifting."

"What are you saying?"

"Just be careful."

"Careful?"

"Who here knows you understand and speak Italian, Gabriela?"

I feel my face heat up. "Only you."

"Keep it that way."

He walks to a cabinet and opens it. I haven't looked inside that one yet and I see now it's a liquor cabinet. He takes out a bottle of whiskey and pours one. He turns to me and extends it.

I shake my head so he closes the cabinet then returns to sit on the sofa across from my chair.

"Who was the man you recognized?" he asks, crossing one ankle over the opposite knee as he sips his drink.

"I didn't recognize anyone," I lie because I haven't figure out how to handle this yet.

"Don't you want to find out who did this to you?"

"Yes, of course."

"Come here, Gabriela." He sits up so both feet are on the floor, and points to the space between his legs.

"Why?"

"Because I said so."

I get up, walk over to him.

He takes my wrist and pulls me closer so I'm standing

between his wide-spread legs. He leans back against the couch, sips his drink and watches me.

"Take off your dress."

"Why?" My heart pounds, blood throbs loud like a drum in my head.

"I want to see you. See if you're ready."

"Ready for what?"

"You know what," he says.

I do. Time for a reckoning.

He sets his drink down and stands.

I try to take a step backward, but the backs of my knees hit the ottoman and I almost fall, but Stefan catches me easily and holds tight to one arm, his expression hardening. He's so close, I feel the heat coming off him, smell the scent of him and some part of me, it wants to curl into him. To have him hold me again like he did when he carried me out of that well. Out of that house.

But what he does is so opposite.

With his free hand, he unzips the dress and strips it off me.

"Step out."

I look down and realize what he means. Step out of the puddle of the dress. I do and he shoves it aside. I cover my breasts.

He sits back down and picks up his drink again, casual as his gaze glides over me.

"Bra off."

"Why?" I ask again, beginning to shudder a little.

"You ask a lot of questions."

"I don't see why you need me to take my bra off."

"Don't make me get up again."

He's seen me naked before. He's touched me. Why is this hard?

"And don't make me repeat myself."

"I just don't understand—"

"I've coddled you," he says, setting his drink down again. This time, instead of standing, he tugs me down by my wrist so I'm leaning into him. He reaches around to my back to unhook the bra. A moment later, it's falling onto his lap.

He releases me and I cover my breasts again.

He looks at the bra, then sets it aside. "Arms at your sides."

"Stefan—"

"Arms at your sides. And whatever you do, don't fucking cry. Don't be a baby."

I swallow back my tears, bury the twisting inside me, that feeling of betrayal.

Why do I feel betrayed, though? He is my enemy. Why do I seem to constantly forget that? He only rescued me because I'm not worth anything to him dead.

I let my arms drop and I force myself to stare at him, my hands fisting, even as he blurs with the build-up of tears because I can't just stop them. Emotions don't work that way, but he wouldn't know that because you'd have to be human to know and he's made of stone.

"Good," he says.

I swipe the back of my hand across my eyes, wipe away those stupid tears.

He looks me over, pausing on the healing bruises as if taking inventory. He reaches to take my wrist.

I try to tug it away, but he holds tight and just gives a shake of his head.

He pulls me down so I'm sitting on his right thigh. I cover myself again with my free arm. He takes that wrist too and holds both in one hand, turning them upward. And when he touches me, trailing his fingers from wrist to elbow and back, it's with a feather-light touch and it's so soft, the contact makes me physically shudder.

"I can be gentle, Gabriela. And I want to be gentle with you."

My nipples are hard, and I want to say it's because I'm cold. He sees too and having him here fully dressed and me in my underwear, it makes me feel exposed and wholly vulnerable.

He shifts my wrists so they're behind my back, keeps them in one of his giant hands. His eyes are locked on mine.

I can't read him. Can't read what he's going to do. I just know he's going to do something.

"But if you don't deserve gentle," he starts, cupping his free hand around the back of my head, fingers massaging my scalp for a moment before they make a fist in my hair.

I make a sound as he tugs. His expression remains level. Hard.

"Then you force me to be rough," he says, slowly pushing me down over his other knee so my face is in the seat of the couch and my legs are trapped between his thighs, my ass in the air.

He releases his grip on my hair and I feel his hand on me, feel him slide my panties between my butt cheeks, exposing me fully. Then, as if to demonstrate what he means, he gives me eight sharp spanks on one cheek.

I don't know if it's the shock or the sting or the sound of it, but it takes me a moment to find my voice, to cry out.

"Stop!" I try to free my wrists, but he's got an iron grip around them and I'm not even sure it's taking any effort for him to keep me pinned like this.

"Do you remember my warning from the other night?" he asks as he begins to rub the spot he just spanked. That part feels good, him rubbing out the pain.

"What are you doing?" I ask, turning my cheek into the couch so I can see his face.

He drags his gaze from my ass to my eyes.

"Getting the truth out of you."

Keeping our eyes locked, he raises his hand and brings it down again, just once on the same spot.

I grunt. It stings. "Stop, please."

"Are you ready to tell me the truth?"

"What truth? What are you—"

He delivers eight more smacks on the opposite cheek and I'm whimpering, gasping for breath by the time he's done.

"Let's get these out of the way," he says, shifting his grip to drag my panties down, releasing me from the trap of his thighs only momentarily as he lets them drop to my ankles so I'm naked. Naked and bent over his knee.

I turn my face into the couch and tug at my wrists. I try opening my hands when I can't free them to cover my ass because I'm sure he can see everything.

"Look at me," he says.

I shake my head. I'm embarrassed and hurt, and a part of me hates him for doing this to me.

"Gabriela, I said look at me."

I suck in a shuddering breath.

In reply he brings his hand down in the center of my ass, making me arch and twist in my effort to get away from him.

"Look. At. Me." He's not even a little winded and I think he can do this all night long. He probably enjoys it.

I turn my cheek into the couch and force myself to meet his eyes. "Why are you hurting me?"

"Because you force my hand."

"I don't...I—"

"I can make you feel good. I *want* to make you feel

good," he says, rubbing my butt again. He makes circles on one cheek, then the other. I calm down a little and his hand slides to the tops of my thighs.

I bite my lip, holding my breath because this touch, the look in his eyes, it's different.

He never shifts his gaze from mine while his fingers travel to my center, to touch me lightly, like he's testing. I realize then what I feel against my belly, it's him.

He's aroused.

And as little sense as it makes, so am I.

His hand is gone for a moment, wrapping around the inside of my thigh and I feel wetness from his fingers—my wetness—as he guides my legs apart, just a little, just enough.

I press the balls of my feet into the carpet. I don't move as he shifts his gaze to my ass. His fingers slide up along my pussy, through the wet folds and up, just touching my other hole before sliding back down. My back arches involuntarily when they brush my clit.

"Gabriela," he starts, and I realize I've closed my eyes. "Look at me, Gabriela."

I shake my head, eyes tightly shut.

He slides a finger back up to my asshole and holds it there. I'm mortified and turned on and I can't seem to breathe.

"Open your eyes and look at me." He brushes his finger over tight hole.

My face burns as I open them to find his eyes on me, darker now, pupils dilated.

He slides his fingers down to my pussy again, rubs a moment longer. Him touching me, it's different than when I touch myself. Better. He softens his hold on my wrists, lets me slip them from his grip.

"Put your hands underneath you and don't move."

I should fight him. Push him off. Tell him to go to hell. But instead, I put my hands underneath myself like he said and watch as with his free hand, he rubs one cheek, then spreads me open.

I'm embarrassed and aroused as he shifts his gaze down and his fingers are moving in my folds, circling my clit.

"You're beautiful," he says, drawing his hand away, turning me, sliding me to the floor between his legs so I'm kneeling there.

He cups one hand on the back of my head to draw me up. He kisses me while he slides his other hand down over the seam of my sex to cup me, to rub. When he bites my lip, I open my mouth and my breathing comes in gasps as he slips his tongue inside my mouth and his finger inside my sex and I think this is the most intimate, erotic thing. This. Connected like this. Him and me. Close. So close.

His thumb circles my nub, presses against it. The finger inside me hurts a little but then it's gone and he's rubbing my clit and I think I'm going to come.

He shifts his mouth to my ear and my hands are squeezing his thighs, my body arching into his palm. Moving against him.

"That's good, Gabriela. Like that. You're so wet."

I tilt my face up. I want to kiss him again. I want him to kiss me.

He must know because he smiles down at me and when he does kiss me it's more a sucking of my lower lip than a kiss. I close my eyes and taste him, and I hear myself, my gasps and sighs. And when I slide my hand up along his thigh, I can feel him.

"I want to taste you," he whispers, and my eyes flutter open as he draws his hand from between my legs and lifts me to lay me back on the ottoman. He spreads my legs and drops down between my knees. With his fingers on either side of my pussy, he opens and looks at me for a long time and him looking at me like this, it makes me feel so strange and all I can do is watch him as he takes me in.

"Stefan," I start, but I stop because I don't know what I'm going to say.

"You are so beautiful," he says.

He runs his chin over my clit, making me gasp at the rough feel of stubble and the instant his mouth closes over it, I gasp, the sensation foreign, his mouth wet and soft and when he begins to suck that hard little nub, I cry out, reaching for him, gripping his hair to pull him closer as my thighs squeeze around him and I come. I come hard, harder than I've ever come and I think I'm saying his name. I think that's me saying his name again and again and again, gasping it, desperate, like I'm gasping for life's breath.

I don't know when he finally lifts me onto his lap. I don't remember him doing that, but he's cradling me, and I'm limp in his arms, my head against his chest and this is what I want. For him to hold me like this. Safe and sound. Protected.

"I like how you taste," he says. He tilts my face up with one finger beneath my chin and kisses my lips. I taste myself on him and I want more. More of him. My hand slides to his stomach, to the hard muscle of it. He takes my wrist and pushes it lower and I blink my eyes open to look at him when he closes my hand around himself over his jeans.

He's big. Big and thick.

"Squeeze," he tells me.

I do and he makes a sound and the way he looks at me, it's dark and dirty and it makes me want him more.

"I want you to say my name like that every time you come," he says, his voice a hoarse breath against my ear.

I close my eyes, not sure what I feel. So many things.

He tucks me closer into him, wrapping his strong arms around me, and I rest my head against his chest and think how I wish I could stay here forever, like this.

When he rests his hand against my thigh, I open my eyes and look at that hand. It's the one he spanked me with. The one he touched me with.

That's what I'm thinking when he interrupts me.

"We have some business to settle between us."

My reckoning.

I turn my gaze up to his.

"Are you ready to answer my questions or do I need to take you back over my knee?" he asks.

We're not finished yet. Did I think for a second, we were? That he'd given up asking me questions I don't want to answer?

I shake my head.

"Good." He draws back and I try to burrow into him, but he pulls away and I'm suddenly cold.

When he perches me on the ottoman, he keeps his hands on my knees and I look at his watch, big and masculine and his hands, big, too.

What did Rafa tell me? To stay in his good graces? I understand that as I look at those hands and remind myself of what he can do with them—good and bad.

I give a shake of my head to clear the fog from my brain. What am I doing?

"Eyes on me, Gabriela," he says.

I look up at him, at his mouth, it takes all I have to not look away. What did he just do? What did I just let him do?

I hug my arms to myself, shivering, and I sit there, mute.

Who am I? I'm a fighter. I don't cower to men. And yet, here I am and look at me now. Naked and trembling.

But this game Stefan is playing, it's new to me. And he's a pro. I'm out of my element. So far out of my league.

"Were you in Rafa's car when he was sideswiped?" he asks.

No point in lying anymore. I have no loyalty to Rafa, after all. "You know the answer, or you wouldn't ask the question."

"Answer me anyway."

Silence.

"Is that where the bump on your forehead came from?"

I blink, not denying, not affirming.

"Words. Tell me now."

"Yes." He knows. It's not news to him. It can't matter anymore.

"The man at the well, who was he?"

"He was the one who sideswiped us. One of them, at least. There were two cars. One on each side."

"Where were you?"

"Taormina."

"Why?"

I shake my head. "He invited me along. It was after you and I...after our fight." I look at this hand, the one I sliced open with my stolen knife. It's healed mostly. I wonder if it will leave a scar, though. I shift my gaze back to his. "He said he had a meeting and felt bad that I was cooped up. We had lunch. We were on our way back when it happened."

He doesn't like this. I can see it in his eyes, in his posture.

"Meeting with whom?" His eyes narrow a little.

"Can I get dressed? I'm cold."

He looks around, gets up, picks up a throw from the arm

of a chair and wraps it around my shoulders, then resumes his seat.

"Meeting with whom?"

"I don't know. I stayed on the beach."

"Unprotected?" Now he looks pissed.

"No, there were two men."

"But he took you there without soldiers?"

"I don't want to get him in trouble, Stefan."

He gets up, shakes his head and runs a hand through his hair, and I think how just moments ago, I had my hands in that hair, was gripping handfuls of it and pulling him to me.

"Did he tell you not to tell me?"

This question, it's the one I don't want to answer.

"Gabriela?"

I nod. "He was just doing something nice."

His jaw tightens and when he resumes his seat, I see the effort it takes him to keep his voice controlled and calm, even though I know calm is about the farthest thing from what he is.

"Rafa isn't nice, Gabriela. Don't you know that yet?"

"I do know that, Stefan, but I also know he's here when you're not. When you just lock me up here. I don't know why you brought me if it was only to lock me away on my own."

He looks confused for a moment, then one side of his mouth curves upward and he snorts.

"What do you think this is exactly?"

I don't answer him. This is Stefan the jerk. This is a whole other side of Stefan to the man who carried me out of that well and it hurts to hear him now. To hear him like this after everything.

He leans back and the look on his face, that, too, hurts. Twists something inside me.

"Do you make up stories? Make yourself the princess in the tower? Locked away by the beast?"

I feel so small and I have nothing to say.

"Maybe you are that. And I admit I'm more beast than prince. But you don't really fantasize that I'll be a doting husband, do you? That we'll play house? Please tell me you're not falling in love with me, Gabriela."

My face burns and I look away. I hug my arms to myself.

No. Never. Never that.

I hate him.

I hate Stefan Sabbioni.

I just need to remember that. To channel that hate. Use it like a weapon, like he does.

Who are you? A voice in my head asks sharply.

This is where my upbringing comes in handy. This part I can do. I'm not so out of my element now. I can hate with the best of them.

"You asked me a question. I answered it. That's all." My tone is flat, forceful almost.

He rubs his hand over his mouth. "Yeah. You did." He retrieves my dress, returns to me. "Arms up," he says.

"I can dress myself."

"Arms up."

"I'm not a fucking doll."

He grips my jaw and pulls me up so I'm half sitting, half standing. "Watch your fucking mouth. Arms. Up."

"So you can say what you like, but I have to watch my mouth?"

"Maybe I need to spank you again. For real, this time." He hardens his grip but I take it. I grit my teeth and take it. "Do you want that, Gabriela? Tell me. Do you want to feel what it will feel like when I spank you for real? Because what I've done up until now is child's play."

"Let go." I say, feeling the stupid fall of tears.

He shakes his head. "Tears don't move me. Have you not figured that out yet?"

"Just let me go." My voice breaks and I sniffle back a sob. I hate him. I hate him so much.

"Then raise your arms so I can dress you."

My arms shake as I do it, and he releases my jaw and slips the dress over my head.

"Stand up."

I look up at him, and all I can think is how alone I am. How completely alone. Why does it feel worse now than it did before? I've always been alone. Why does it hurt so much now?

"Why didn't you just leave me in that well? You should have."

At that he pauses, and I swear that for one split second, I see that other Stefan. The one who came for me, who climbed into that well to carry me out. The one who swore he wouldn't let anyone hurt me again.

I want that Stefan. I need him. And that is the worst part of this.

I turn away when more tears fall. I don't wipe my eyes fast enough though because one drops to my knee and I know he sees. I feel so small, so incredibly, stupidly small, that I just sit there and keep wiping at these stupid never-ending tears. And here I thought I was so strong.

"Stop feeling sorry for yourself and get up."

I stand up, using my wrists to wipe my eyes.

He leans in toward me, wraps his big arms around me and I hate myself for wanting to lean in to him. For thinking that he means to hold me. I hate myself for wanting that. For wanting him to fucking hold me.

Because all he does is zip the dress before he steps backward.

He only did what he did to get me to talk. But I don't understand. The spanking, I can see that. Hurt me to make me talk. That's what the mafia does, right? But why the rest? Why tell me he can be gentle? Why did he lay me back on that ottoman and do what he did? Why did he hold me afterwards?

I shake my head, dislodge those thoughts.

He doesn't care about me. That is all I need to remember. I'm sure he's got women lined up to fuck, Clara at the front of that line. What use would he have for an inexperienced virgin who happens to be his enemy's daughter?

"Why did you do that?" I ask

"What?"

"What you just did."

He grins. "Eat your pussy?" I hate that I feel my face burn. "I should take my belt to your ass for running away in the first place, you know that?"

"Why don't you? You'd like that, right? I felt how hard you were when you spanked me. Is that what gets you off? Hurting women? Overpowering them to hurt them?"

He steps closer, the look on his face base, degrading. "Don't forget you got wet when I spanked you."

How can he turn everything around on me? Am I that easy a target?

I spin to go, but he catches my arm.

"I want to go to my room, Stefan."

"One more question."

I don't have a choice, so I wait for it.

"Who put the marks on your back?"

"You already know that too."

"Say it."

"I hate you."

"Say it."

"Why?"

"Because I want to hear it."

"My father did! My father. All right? Happy?"

He pauses like he's really considering that question. "Not really, no." He doesn't release me.

"Let me go. Please, Stefan, just let me go. I want to go."

"Away from me."

I nod. It's what I want, right?

It takes him a moment, but when he releases me, I bend to pick up my panties.

He steps on them, blocking me from taking them.

"I'll keep those," he says.

It takes me a moment, but I leave them and straighten. "Whatever, pervert." I walk to the door. I'm twisting the doorknob when he calls out my name.

"Gabriela."

I stop. I don't look back. I'm not sure how much more of this I can take. Because what the hell just happened in here?

"Tomorrow is Alex's memorial service. I thought you'd want to go."

At that, I turn. Does he mean to take me?

"Do you?" he asks.

I nod, but I'm cautious. I don't want to get my hopes up, but I would do anything to go.

"Car leaves at nine."

5

STEFAN

Once she's gone, I sit back down and pick up my whiskey. I drink it, lean my head back.

Rafa.

My cousin has lied to me before. I know he lies. This particular lie bugs me.

The question, though, isn't that he lied but why? Is it because he knew I'd be pissed that he took Gabriela out of the house without protection or permission? Or is it something more?

As far as who he met with, I would be surprised if it was anyone other than his father.

Francesco Catalano was a gracious host to me these last couple of days. I went to personally thank him not because I'm stupid enough to think he helped me out of the goodness of his heart. Gabriela's question about how he knew, well, that's my question too. It's too fucking convenient that some of his people overheard the men from that boat bragging about what they'd done. Way too convenient.

Francesco is my mother's sister's husband. He isn't blood.

My father never liked Francesco. Never trusted him. He's not Sicilian born, for one thing, and with my father, that alone was enough. But there was more than that and if there's one thing I learned from my father it's to always trust your gut.

But my father did love my mother and he loved her family. My aunt Gina, Rafa's mother, and my father were good friends. He met my mom through Gina. Gina lived with us before I was born. The three of them were all close. She came to my father if she needed advice and all my father had to do to make sure Gina took that advice—even when it wasn't asked for—was raise an eyebrow.

It was for her that he gave Francesco responsibility over one of our most profitable routes north. And when the first shipment came in short, he turned a blind eye. For her. But then it happened again. And again after that.

He could never prove it was Francesco, though, and Francesco always had an answer.

I've never felt particularly close to my uncle. Honestly, I've never liked the man. But Rafa and I grew up best friends. I think that was because Gina spent more time here with Rafa than at her own home in Taormina.

What I told Gabriela about the constantly shifting line between ally and enemy, I've watched it play out multiple times over my lifetime. I'm watching it play out now.

Rafa. Where do your loyalties lie, cousin?

I finish my drink, put the glass down and look at the ring on my finger. Our family ring. Passed down from father to son. It was supposed to have gone to Antonio.

I twist it. Think about each of them. Each dead and in his grave now.

When I get up to get more whiskey, I see that photo album. Instead of going for the whiskey, I pick it up and sit down in the chair where Gabriela had been reading when I came in. I open it, leaf slowly through the pages.

Strange that so many people pictured in this album are dead. I miss them. I miss my family.

My mom used to say that no one would love you like a mother loves her children.

That thought makes me think of Gabriela. Of what she'd said about her mother's drowning. Of what I know.

I think about what I said to her just now. What an asshole thing to say. To do.

Her words come back to me, her voice almost an echo.

"Why didn't you just leave me in that well? You should have."

I get that whiskey now. Drink it in one swallow.

What I feel for her is strange. Not what I expected or thought. Is that why I was such a dick just now? Spanking her to get the truth, that I'll do again if I have to. Playing with her, though, laying her down to eat her pussy, I shouldn't have done that. Shouldn't have touched her like that. Shouldn't have made those comments about the tower. About playing house. She's young and inexperienced, and I'm not fighting fair.

After what happened, it would be normal for her to feel some sort of affection or at least attachment to me. I saved her life. I rescued her.

Princess in the tower.

Princess in a well.

And I mocked her. Put her back in her place after stripping her naked and getting a taste of her.

Or was I redrawing the lines between us for my own sake?

Because the way she makes me feel, this possessiveness that burns inside me when I look at her, think about her, it's not supposed to be this way.

I put my glass down and make my way to the door. This line of thinking is going nowhere. She's mine to do with as I please. That's what it all comes down to where she's concerned. That's *all* it comes down to.

My business with her father, it's my business with her father. Not her.

She's a pawn and it's not like she doesn't know that. And I'll use her as I see fit and she will be my wife and if I want to strip her naked and eat her pussy, I will. I will do much more than that.

I spy her panties on the floor and bend to pick them up. I bring them to my nose and inhale.

I'm hard again and tuck the panties into my pocket before heading up to my room, pausing only briefly when I pass her door. I hear the shower. She's probably washing my scent from her. My touch from her.

I should tell her it's pointless. I'll only mark her again tomorrow.

6

STEFAN

The next morning, she's downstairs and ready to go by quarter-to-nine. She's wearing a somber black dress. Her hair is piled into a neat bun at the top of her head, her bangs secured behind her ear. She's wearing a little make-up, cover up to hide the remaining bruises and lip gloss, and is standing by the door fidgeting when I get downstairs.

She walks up to me as soon as I'm on the first-floor landing. "Is my brother in danger?" she blurts out.

I'm surprised by this question. Actually, I'm more surprised she didn't ask it sooner. "Your brother is safe. I have soldiers placed there."

"You do?" She looks confused. Disbelieving.

"Yes. He's safe."

"Why didn't you tell me?"

"It didn't come up."

She turns away, scratches her head, then shifts her gaze back to mine. "Thank you."

"This falls in the good category," I say. "You just behave yourself and it can always be like this."

Her mood shifts, a flash of anger crossing her features, but it's gone as quickly as it came.

"The dress looks good on you."

She meets my gaze, gives me a cold once-over. "I'm ready to go."

"You say thank you when someone gives you a compliment."

"We're going to a memorial service for my friend who is dead because of me. I realize you could care less, but I'm not fishing for compliments. It was the only thing I had in my closet that was appropriate."

Her eyes glisten and I see the circles beneath them that she's tried to cover up.

"He made a choice," I say. "What happened to him is not your fault."

"I don't need you to tell me that." She puts on a brave face, but I can see how fragile that surface layer is. "Can we go?"

I gesture to the man at the front door and he opens it. Gabriela flinches when I set my hand at her lower back and guide her out to the waiting SUV. We drive in silence to the airport and within two hours, are making our way up the steps to the small church in a suburb of Rome for the memorial service.

The parking lot is full, and people talk quietly as they climb the stairs and pass the heavy, wooden door to each other. Organ music plays a melancholy, gothic tune. Music for a funeral.

I breathe in the smell of incense already heavy in the air and it takes me back to when I was younger. To when we would attend mass as a family.

We weren't welcome in the small church then. I felt it even as a little boy.

And neither Gabriela nor I are welcome here now.

I see it in the faces that turn in our direction as I walk her up the aisle and into an empty pew.

A glance at her tells me she sees it too.

"Are you okay?" I ask her. I don't know why.

She shrugs away from me. "You should go. You don't belong here."

"Do you?" I ask, gesturing to the family who are openly talking about us from the front pews.

"I used to," she says, sitting down and picking up the memory card.

I glance at it, see Alex smiling back. See her lightly touch his hair in the picture and I'm pissed. I'm pissed that this happened. That we're here for this. The kid shouldn't have died.

"Haven't you done enough?" asks a man.

Gabriela tilts her face up, and what I see in her eyes, it brings out something dark inside me. Dark and fiercely protective.

I turn to face the man. He's in his forties I'd guess. Not the father, I know he's dead. Maybe an uncle?

"You are?" I ask politely because we're at a fucking memorial service.

"Alex's uncle, not that it's any of your business, Sabbioni." Ah, he knows me. Saves me the trouble of introducing myself.

But he looks past me to Gabriela who's stood up.

"I didn't...Alex was..." Gabriela stammers.

I shift my posture, blocking Gabriela from the uncle as I step out into the aisle. He's a big guy, but so am I, and if he thinks he's going to somehow make us leave, he's got another thing coming.

"She has as much right to be here as you. Gabriela and Alex were good friends."

"And look where that got Alex." He gives me a once-over, then peers around me. "Is your father coming too?" he spits the words.

I put a hand on his shoulder, squeeze. "Watch yourself. We're in a fucking church. I advise you to go back to your pew and sit down. We're staying."

The man leans against my hand as he gets his face in mine. "Leave."

"Stefan," Gabriela starts, her hand on my arm.

"Sit down, Gabriela," I tell her without turning away.

"Maybe we should—"

"You're making a scene," I tell the man.

He looks around, notes all the eyes on us, backs up a step. "You leave your men outside, Sabbioni."

"Do you see my men inside?"

His eyes narrow.

"You lost your nephew," I say. "My fiancée's lost her friend. She grieves as you do. Now go back to your seat and let her be."

He grits his teeth, looks at Gabriela once more before scanning the dead silent church, all eyes on us, all ears on us. He then returns to his pew at the front.

Gabriela is still standing, her face white, a rosary in one hand, the memorial card in the other and all I can think is how different she is to who she was when I first met her two years ago. When I first started this.

And I think how little I like this change.

Because she is being buried. And if not buried, then at the very least, she's breaking.

The music changes, the boom of the organ commanding our attention. The procession of altar boys begins to make their way up the aisle, followed by a priest swinging the smoking censer, all of it so familiar and yet so far out of reach, as if the past never was at all.

That's the thing with time. I wonder if it wouldn't be better to forget. To set fire to all the photographs. To somehow burn all the memories.

"Thank you," Gabriela whispers, drawing me to the present.

I nod and take my place beside her in our pew.

7

GABRIELA

I think Stefan is bipolar. At the very least he has multiple personalities.

Throughout the service, as I pass my fingers over the rosary beads Miss Millie lent me, he sits quietly attentive, giving the impression he's listening to the mass when I know he's just watching me and everyone else.

I don't know Alex's uncle. I've seen him once, but I don't even know his name. Alex and his father were the only ones out of his family to work for my father. But if I'd been on my own and he came to tell me to leave, I'd have left. I wouldn't know how to say no, to stand up to him the way Stefan did.

It's so confusing being with him. One minute he's a fierce protector. The next, he's the predator and I'm the prey. And I feel like I don't know when either will take over.

The service lasts two hours and afterwards, as we walk out of the church, I feel drained. Weepy.

"We'll get lunch before we go back," Stefan says as he helps me into the SUV.

I know we're close to his uncle's house and I really don't want to go there. Or anywhere, really.

"Can we just go home?" Why do I keep referring to it as home? It's not my home. "I don't feel like company."

"It's just us. You don't have to be anything with me."

"Oh. I assumed you'd want to see your uncle."

He shakes his head. "I didn't think you'd feel very social after this."

Well, that was considerate. I bite the inside of my cheek and we don't speak again until we're seated at a quiet restaurant in a part of the city I've never been to. We're the only customers and a bartender, a waiter and two other men are nearby to wait only on us.

"Thank you for bringing me to the service," I say. I know he didn't have to do that.

"You're welcome."

He picks up my menu and hands it to me.

I take it, open it and scan the page, just picking the first item I see, then close it again and set it down. I don't care what I eat.

Stefan takes his time, though. Is this what it will be like with us? Will we sit quietly, awkwardly like this? Or will he ship me off somewhere once we're married? Resume his life?

Resume.

That makes the assumption he's stopped living the life he's always lived.

My hands in my lap, I finger the diamond on my left hand, feel the weight of it.

My new life. This is it. And I have no more control over it than I did my old one.

But I'm going to do what Stefan told me last night. I'm taking his advice. I'd tell him if I didn't think he'd get cocky but I'm going to stop feeling sorry for myself. I've become weak since this began. And since the kidnapping, I feel like I don't know who I am anymore.

As if Stefan feels this shift in my mood, he closes his menu and looks at me with those strange, hazel eyes.

I think of his eyes on me last night. Think of how I looked to him when he touched me.

Heat flushes through me, settling at my core.

What he did to me last night, I want it again. And I'm determined to learn this game fast and learn it well, because I have to beat him at it. Let him underestimate me. Let him think I'm laughable. A child. I know what I felt when I touched him. He wants me. And that is a weakness.

The waiter is at our table a moment later and Stefan asks a few questions, then asks me if I'm ready to order.

I open my menu again because I'd forgotten what it was and order the first pasta dish listed.

"That's all?" Stefan asks.

"That's all."

He orders a starter and a main course as well as a bottle of wine. Once the wine comes, the waiter pours for both of us and we drink a sip.

"I want to see my brother," I blurt out.

"Your brother's in New York."

"You have a jet."

He takes a deep breath in, studying me. "We'll talk about it."

"No. I want to see him. Especially now."

"You have the phone. You can FaceTime him anytime."

"It's not the same. And he doesn't understand why I haven't been there. I used to go every week, twice whenever I could. Please, Stefan. I just want this one thing." I pause. "I'll do something you want in exchange."

He sighs.

"Anything," I add.

"Let's talk about it later."

"No, not later. Now."

"If you push me, the answer is no. Let me think about it."

There's a long silence while we study one another.

I sigh. "Why were you like that last night?"

"Like what?"

"Mean."

He makes a face, like he's going to laugh or say something cutting, but I speak first and cut him off.

"Don't tell me to grow up. You don't have to be a jerk to me."

"You lied to me. How do you want me to be when you lie to me?"

"The thing with Rafa, I should have told you. At least when I recognized the man at that house. I get that you were mad, but the rest, the things you said, I'm not my father. Don't hate me for his sins."

"I don't hate you, Gabriela."

"That's the thing. Sometimes, I feel like you do. Then other times, it's like you're this other person. The one who carried me up out of that well."

"Which one do you want?"

His question catches me off guard and it takes me a moment to process because he seems genuine.

Don't be a fool.

I give a shake of my head. Am I so desperate for affection? He's just fucking with me.

"My father said there's a modification to the contract. What is it?"

"Which one do you want?" he repeats.

The waiter brings his starter and sets it down. Stefan doesn't take his eyes off me for a second.

I, on the other hand, look at anything but him.

"Which one, Gabriela?" he probes.

I look up at him and my heart is racing and the thoughts in my head, I don't understand them.

"The one who carried me up out of that well."

I say it. I put it out there and I don't know if he's setting me up, if he just wants to make fun of me or hurt me somehow but I feel too weak to fight him today. I don't know what he gets out of it, anyway. What pleasure he can have from making fun of me. Maybe he's just a sadist.

He looks thoughtful, though, not mocking.

But he still doesn't speak.

I pick up my glass, swallow some wine, clear my throat and wait, regretting having said it out loud.

It's a long time before he finally says something. "I would not have left you in that well. What you said last night, that I should have left you there, I wouldn't." He drinks a sip of his wine, then puts his glass down. "But I'm not what you think, Gabriela. And you should remember that one heroic act does not a hero make."

"I know what you are, Stefan. I know who you are. I remember you from the first night in my bedroom. That's you. The real you."

"And who is that?"

"Someone broken. Someone alone."

"Like you?"

8

STEFAN

She's quiet for the rest of the day, throughout lunch and the flight back to Palermo. It's late afternoon when we're back and as soon as we walk inside, Gabriela heads for the stairs.

"Gabriela."

She stops, turns to me.

There's so much sadness in her eyes right now that it's hard to look at her. To see her like this. Alex's death pushed her over the edge, but this has been building for a long time. Maybe all her life.

It's everything that's already happened to her.

All the things that are still happening. That have yet to happen.

"Go change into something comfortable. I want to take you somewhere." As I say it, I'm not sure why I'm going to do it. I've been to Skull Rock once since Antonio betrayed us. It was the night I buried what was left of him.

She opens her mouth to protest. I can already hear it before she even says a word.

I go to her, put my finger to her lips. "You said you'd do anything if I let you see your brother."

"You're going to take me to see Gabe?" she seems surprised and when she smiles, her eyes sparkle for the first time in days.

I smile too. "Not right this second, but yes. First, change. And bring a sweater. Hurry."

"Okay."

She disappears up the stairs and I follow her to do the same, putting on a pair of jeans and a T-shirt. It's a few minutes after I'm downstairs that she follows wearing a pair of shorts and a tank top and is tying a sweater around her hips.

I hold out my hand.

She looks at it cautiously, but slips hers inside mine and a few minutes later, I'm leading her out the back of the house and down those stone steps to the cove.

"Where are we going?" she asks as I help her down. The stairs are steep, and I wonder how she managed them in the dark that night without falling.

"Have you ever swum in the sea under the moon?" I ask her as we step onto the sandy beach.

She pulls back, her expression changing.

"Stefan, I can't swim. You know that."

"You can swim. You're just afraid to and I already told you I'm not going to let anything happen to you." This is one reason I didn't tell her to put a suit on. She'd have given me trouble.

She's reluctant as I guide her around a corner, following the shoreline to a hidden cove I'm sure she hasn't discovered yet.

"I used to play here with my brother growing up," I say as we turn a final corner where my boat is docked. "Now the toys are a little different." It's a sailboat, not a very big one, just what I need. I haven't taken it out in a while.

Gabriela looks up at it, at the high sails, the beautiful polished wood.

"It belonged to my father. I inherited it." It's well maintained, even through the years I wasn't able to do it myself.

She turns to me. "You can sail?"

I nod. "Have you ever been sailing?"

"A long time ago. With my mom and brother."

"Well," I start gesturing to the boat. "Then you can help."

It takes a little doing to convince her to get on and I don't really expect her to help with the sails but not ten minutes later, we're out on the water having caught the wind and are sailing steadily toward what Antonio and I named Skull Rock. It feels like a lifetime ago that we did that. It is a lifetime. A whole other life.

I sit beside Gabriela as we watch the sun set on the horizon and she slips her sweater on, pulling the sleeves over her hands as the breeze cools a little and when I shift closer and put an arm around her, she doesn't pull away.

"I'm not sure what's more beautiful," she starts. "The sunsets or the sunrises."

"Maybe it depends on the day. If you need a beginning or an ending."

The moon replaces the sun in the sky. It's full and the night is clear.

I work the sails and navigate the boat to Skull Rock and a little while later, I lift her out of the boat. We walk onto the shore where we sit on the sand and look back at the house, at Palermo in the distance, and the moonlit water. The only sound is that of the water lapping against the boat, waves gently rolling onto the beach.

"What is this place?" she asks.

"Skull Rock. At least that's what my brother and I named it. Look," I lean close to her, point. "Close your right eye and look at the rock. Tell me it doesn't look like a human skull."

"That's creepy."

"Yep. Exactly what we liked when we were little."

"I saw a picture of you when you were little. You were cute. And fat."

I can hear a smile in her voice. I smile too. "I never passed up a plate of my mom's homemade pasta," I say with a wink.

Her smile fades a moment later and she lies down on her back to look up at the sky.

I watch her. She's so fucking beautiful. Even like this, sad and pale, she's still the most beautiful thing I've ever seen.

"Do you miss her?" she asks.

"I miss them all."

She glances at me but shifts her gaze back to the sky. "Do you believe in Heaven and Hell, Stefan?"

I lie down too, hands behind my head, and think about her question. Think how to answer her.

"Yes and no."

She turns her head to look at me. "What do you mean?"

"I believe in hell. I believe that's where we're left when they die."

"That's so sad." Her eyes glisten with tears and one slides over her temple.

I wipe it away. "You cry too much."

"Please don't call me a baby and ruin this."

She must see confusion on my face.

"You're being nice, Stefan. Don't mess it up."

"I wasn't going to call you a baby." I turn on my side, set

my elbow on the sand and lean my head in my hand. "What do you believe?"

She shifts her gaze up. "I think those stars are us. When we die. I think they're our souls. And I think you're right about hell being right here."

Her voice breaks on more tears. A torrent of them.

"Gabi," I say, not sure why I use that abbreviated version of her name.

She tries to pull away, but I don't let her. Instead, I turn her to face me and I lean down to kiss one of those tears. I taste the salt of them and when I've kissed them all away, I set my forearms on either side of her face. She looks up at me, her hands on my shoulders.

"Everyone I love is dead. Everyone but Gabe. And he's... he's not..."

"Shh." I lift her to me, hug her, holding her tight as she dissolves into tears. If I let her go, I wonder if she'll disappear. Melt into her pain. "You may be broken, but you're not alone. You don't have to be, at least."

She turns her head away, shakes it, pushes at me to get up.

"Don't push me away," I say, not letting her go.

"One heroic act does not a hero make," she says, repeating my words from earlier.

We just stay like that for a long minute. Then, without asking, I begin to undress her. I didn't bring her out here to watch her cry. I brought her to stop the tears.

When she resists, I tell her to be quiet. I leave her bra and panties on and stand to strip off my clothes. I then lift her up and carry her into the water.

"Stefan, no!" She clings to me and struggles against me at once.

"Yes." I hold tight to her and she gasps as I walk in deeper. "I won't let you go. I promise."

"I can't."

"You can."

"I'm scared."

I stop when the water comes up to my chest and she's partly in it. The sea is cool and calm. "Do you trust me?"

She looks up at me and I know I've given her no reason to trust me. The opposite.

"Do you *want* to trust me?" I rephrase.

She nods and I get the feeling she's desperate to.

I take another step. "Watch the sky, Gabriela, and know that I won't let you go," I tell her as I swim out and she slowly relaxes, loosening her death grip, and, finally, floats.

We stay out there for a long while, neither of us breathing a word and something shifts between us. It swells as I float alongside her, holding her hand, never letting her go. We're weightless out here, both of us weightless, at least for a while.

9

STEFAN

It's midnight when we're back at the house and I carry her to my room. She doesn't resist when I strip off her clothes, her underthings still damp, and put her in the shower under a flow of hot water. I strip too and step in beside her and there's no resistance when I kiss her. When I take her in my arms and kiss her as the water washes sea salt from us.

She opens to me and I cup the back of her head. I don't ever want to stop kissing her. Don't ever want to stop holding her like this.

When the water begins to cool, I switch off the shower and dry her then myself before lifting her up and carrying her to my bed. I lay her down and lie down beside her, shifting so I'm on top of her but keeping most of my weight on my forearms so I don't crush her.

I slide one hand down and cup the mound of her breast. I run my fingernail over her nipple, and she moans into my mouth. When I pull away, it's to look at her.

She licks her lips, reaches up to touch my cheek, slides her hand down to my chest and sets it against my heart.

We don't talk. We don't say a single word. Not for a long while. We just kiss and kiss and look at each other. And I can't get enough of touching her. Tasting her. Can't get close enough to her.

"Christ, Gabriela," I start. "I want you." I roll off her and onto my side to slide my hand down over her belly.

She cups my cheek, touches her mouth to mine. "Kiss me again."

I do.

I do more than that as my fingers slip between her legs and she opens to me and she's wet. Her pussy is as wet as her mouth that I can't stop kissing and I touch her, moving my fingers through her folds, finding the swollen nub of her clit.

I drag my mouth from hers and, leaning my head down, I lick one nipple, then slide my tongue across to the other and back and forth and back and forth before slipping down between her legs, my tongue leaving a wet trail as it travels over her belly button to the seam of her sex, as I push her legs wide and look at her like this. Beautiful and open and mine.

"Stefan," she starts, trying to close her legs.

I put a hand on each thigh and stop her. "Mine," I say. "All mine, Gabriela." I kiss her pussy, lick it, then slide back up to kiss her mouth. "You taste so good."

I take her hand and guide it to myself. And when she grips me, fuck.

Her eyes are wide as she looks at me, at my thick, ready cock. She slides her hand over the tip, smearing pre-cum there.

I close my hand over hers to show her how to move.

"Grip it hard," I say, thinking about how tight her cunt is going to feel when I'm inside her. Wanting so badly to be inside her. "Like this." I move her along my length and I'm pretty sure I can come just watching her watch me and it takes all I have to hold back because fuck, what I want right now is to sink my cock into her wet cunt and feel her virgin blood spill all over me as I make her mine.

I take her wrists in one of my hands and raise her arms over her head to wrap her hands around one of the rungs of the headboard. I kiss her again.

"Keep your hands there. Don't move," I tell her as I move down over her body, my tongue sliding over her center, down to the seam of her sex. I grip both thighs and open her wide, pushing her knees high and in the moonlight coming in from the open balcony doors, I can see all of her, her wet, open cunt, her tight little asshole.

I lean my face down and lick her and her hands are in my hair instantly. I grip her wrists and raise my head.

"What did I tell you?"

"Not to move my hands."

"Do it or I'll take you over my knee and spank you before I make you come."

Her eyes are dark and they glisten in the moon but it's not with tears as she puts her hands back over her head to grip the headboard and I resume my work, circling her clit before sliding my tongue between her folds, licking the space between her pussy and her asshole before circling that tight little hole, too.

"Stefan!" Again, her hands are in my hair.

I get up on my knees, turn her a little, just enough to give her a smack on the ass.

She gasps but this isn't like last night. This is erotic. Last night was punishment, albeit mild.

"You shouldn't—" she starts

"What? I shouldn't what? I can lick your pussy but not your asshole?"

Even in the moonlight, I see her face flush with embarrassment.

I grin, flip her over onto her belly. "Up on your elbows and knees. Spread your legs wide for me. I want your cunt and your asshole open to me, Gabriela, because you're mine. Every part of you is mine."

She's turned on, I see it in her eyes, smell the musk of her arousal in the air. When she moves, I watch her. She lifts her hips high, spreading her knees wide and watching me with her cheek on her forearm. I settle myself between her open legs and spread her ass cheeks wider, look at her, all of her, and I dip my head down and I tongue her asshole again, tongue it and rub her clit between my fingers until she's gasping, her hands fisted, her back arched deeply.

"Stefan. Oh fuck!"

"Come," I command as I swipe my tongue greedily over her cunt and back to her asshole. "Come with my tongue in your asshole and my fingers on your clit."

"Stefan!" she cries out, gasping, bucking with orgasm, panting and whimpering my name over and over and over again.

And fuck.

That.

That chanting of my name. All I can think as she collapses on the bed, breathless, her body jerking with aftershocks, is that I will never get enough of *that*.

I get up on my knees and tug her down the bed by her ankle, then flip her back over and grip one thigh, push it up.

"You like me licking your asshole, Gabriela?" I ask, kissing her.

She nods, kissing me like she's starved.

"Say it."

"I like it," she's out of breath, her eyes only half-open.

"You like what?" I taunt, rubbing my cock between her dripping folds while I watch her.

"You're going to make me come again," she starts, trying to kiss me.

I draw just out of reach. "Say it or I'll stop." I take her hands, weave my fingers through hers and spread her arms wide to look at her like this. "Say it. Tell me how much you liked it when I licked your asshole."

"I loved you licking my...my asshole."

I smile wide. "Good girl." Fuck. "You don't know how badly I want to fuck you right now."

"Yes."

"No. Not yet." I kiss her soft mouth before rising up on my knees. "You're too sweet. Too innocent for me, you know that?" Not that I will let her go.

She leans up on her elbows, looks at me, at my cock in my fist. I let her watch as I smear it through her wet folds, watch her gasp and bite her lip when I rub against her clit.

"Come here, Gabriela," I tell her, cupping the back of her head, as I lean over her, my cock at her face. "Open your mouth."

She opens, sets her little pink tongue to the tip of my cock. I close my eyes and fist the base of it when she circles, licking pre-cum from me before closing her lips around my tip and sucking.

"Fuck." I push deeper but what I want to do is to thrust into her, to fuck her face. Fuck. I want to be balls deep in her sweet little mouth and come down her throat until she chokes on me.

Her hands move to my abdomen, pushing against me.

I look down to see her panicked eyes and I draw out, let

her catch her breath. I settle myself between her legs again, rubbing my cock between her folds before taking it into my fist and pumping, watching her watch me.

"I'm going to come all over you. I'm going to mess up that pretty face of yours. Open your legs wider, let me see you rub your greedy little pussy. Let me see you make yourself come."

She does, sliding her hand between her legs, rubbing her clit with the pad of two fingers and fuck, watching her like this, looking at her face, at her dirty fingers doing their work, hearing her come again, it sends me over the edge.

I come hard, sending ropes of cum across her belly, her breasts, her mouth. I cover her with it, and seeing her like this, seeing her soiled with my seed, it sends a final wave of pleasure through me and I shudder with it, shudder as I empty, as I collapse beside her on my bed.

10

GABRIELA

I wake up to find myself alone in Stefan's bed but there's a note on the nightstand propped up against the lamp. I pick it up to read it.

> *You looked so peaceful I didn't want to wake you.*
> *I'm meeting with one of my lawyers, but I'll be back later.*
>
> *x*
> *Stefan*

I smile, touch the letters, hover over the small 'x'.

Wrapping the sheets around myself, I walk out onto the balcony and to my room, tuck the note into my nightstand drawer and go into the bathroom to shower.

I think about yesterday. How it started, how it ended.

I'm still sad about Alex. I will feel his loss for a long time. And I should. I want to. He was my friend and I will remember him and when we find out who set that fire, I will avenge his death.

But Stefan, what he did, he didn't even have to tell me

about the memorial service. I wouldn't have known. And he certainly didn't have to take me.

This makes for a second heroic act. Do the two combined a hero make?

Instead of a shower, I opt for a bath and I soak for a long time thinking about all the things that have happened in the last few weeks. How much my life has changed. I think about what Stefan told me about being careful and I get the feeling I was wrong about him and Rafa. Maybe he doesn't trust him like I guessed. Maybe the three of them, Rafa, Clara and Stefan aren't the Three Musketeers.

I remember when Clara called Rafa and I heard his side of the conversation. He told her he missed her. Was that just cousins talking? She was swimming naked in Stefan's pool the night they were all here. That's not something cousins do, at least not any cousins I know.

But what I'm thinking makes no sense. If she's having an affair with Rafa, she wouldn't be swimming naked in Stefan's pool with Stefan watching.

What had he said about that? She'd lost a bet? What kind of bet would any woman agree to that would have her stripping off her clothes in front of her male cousins to swim naked?

I shake my head to clear the thoughts of her, of the image of her perfect body, a body like I'll never have. Where she's built like a woman with heavy breasts and perfectly proportioned hips, I'm built more like a boy. Well, okay, not quite a boy. I'm a small B cup on a really good day, but I have a good butt. I just don't have that hourglass figure she does.

When I'm finished with the bath, I get dressed and go downstairs to have a late breakfast. As soon as Stefan is finished with the attorney, I will talk to him about Gabe. Get a date so I can tell my brother when I'm coming to see him.

I guess we need to talk about the wedding too. Will he still want to go through with it? Does what's happening between us change things?

Whoa. Slow down.

What is happening between us? We had sex. Almost.

No, it's not that. He was nice to me. I think he really cared that I was sad. That's why he took me out to Skull Rock. And he heard me at the restaurant. He repeated my words, didn't he? About being broken and alone?

Together, we're not alone. We may both still be broken, but we're not alone.

Warning bells ring in my head.

I'm getting carried away. What did he say about me? That I'm sweet and innocent.

He's a man. I never thought about what he'd do sexually. I never considered that what we'd have would be real. Not that I've had much time to ponder it.

The fact is we didn't even have sex. He wants to wait until we're married. He's weirdly old-fashioned. But no matter what, the fact that he's my first, and just the circumstances around our relationship, it makes sense that I would feel attached to him.

I just have to remember he's experienced. He won't feel the same attachment I'd naturally feel for him.

Collateral damage.

The words ring in my head.

Miss Millie appears with coffee and I shake off the thought.

I don't want to think about this right now. There's nothing to think about. This is all going to play out the way they want it to. By they, I mean my father and Stefan. I have no control over this.

No, that's not true. I have control over one thing. My heart. I can guard it. I have to.

But am I too late already?

"How about some French Toast this morning, Gabriela?" Miss Millie asks and not a moment too soon as that was a dead-end road I was traveling.

"I would love French Toast. Is it okay if I come help? Maybe eat in the kitchen? I don't want to sit here by myself."

She seems confused for a moment but then nods. "Come on with me. I should have suggested it myself. With Stefan gone so much, I don't want you to feel lonely."

"Is he gone again? I thought he was in his study meeting with his lawyer?"

"That's this afternoon. He went to pay Rafa a visit this morning."

"He's visiting Rafa?"

She's walking ahead of me but stops, turns to me and I see on her face that she is thinking she said too much.

"I don't think he'd planned it, dear. Come on, let's get you some breakfast."

"I thought he was here," I mutter, watching her walk ahead of me.

Does he lie so easily? Why didn't he tell me he was going to see Rafa? Because I know what it's about.

Me.

11

STEFAN

Rafa seems surprised when he opens the door and finds me on his doorstep.

"Stef," he starts. His gaze shifts over my shoulder momentarily. Has he always done that and I'm just realizing it? "What are you doing here?"

He's barefoot and bare chested and when I step inside, he buttons the last of the buttons on the jeans he must have just pulled on.

"Dropping in," I say, studying him, eyeing the tattoo over his heart. A symbol of his pledge. His fealty to my family.

He glances toward the bedroom door, seeming anxious.

"Bad time?" I ask.

"No. Of course not. Just have a girl in there," he says. "Come in. Let me go tell her to have a shower and I'll make coffee." He closes the door and I walk through the open plan living area to the kitchen counter while he momentarily disappears into the bedroom. He's back not two minutes later.

"Who is she?"

He shrugs a shoulder. "No one special." He switches on a

burner, fills the bottom of the small espresso pot with water and measures out espresso. He sets the pot over the flame and turns to look at me. "What's up?"

"Does your dad get pissed when he sees that?" I gesture to his tattoo.

He touches the space over his heart, looks down at it. "I don't show him. Easier that way."

"But he knows it's there. Does it piss him off?"

He shrugs a shoulder and busies himself getting two espresso cups. "Doesn't matter, Stefan. I stand behind it."

"Do you?"

He turns back to me, cocks his head to the side. "Something going on?"

"Why didn't you tell me that you took Gabriela to Taormina?"

He gives a short chuckle, like he was waiting for this. "I just felt sorry for her, that's all."

"And that you didn't take soldiers?"

His jaw tightens.

The coffee pot steams and he switches off the burner then pours espresso into two cups. He hands me one and we sit at the counter.

"Any special reason you didn't take soldiers?"

"It's not a big deal, Stef. I didn't think I'd need them."

"Or you didn't want your father to see Sabbioni soldiers in territory he thinks belongs to him?"

"It's not like that. You know that."

"Isn't it?"

He sighs, drinks a sip of espresso, then touches his lip because the liquid is steaming hot.

"Sicily is yours. He knows that. He's not stupid enough to try something like that. He's your uncle, Stefan. He respects that. Respects you."

"My aunt is dead. No reason for loyalty. And when she was alive it was a very fragile bond."

"He just helped you find Gabriela, for fuck's sake. He wouldn't help his enemy. He'd want to weaken you if he was your enemy."

"Or maybe he set it all up to gain my trust.'"

"You're not that stupid and trust doesn't come that easy. He knows that."

I sip my espresso. "How often do you see him?"

He shakes his head like he's trying to remember, but I know him. Rafa doesn't forget a thing. He's just trying to figure out the best way to answer me.

I think about what I told Gabriela. About how that line between ally and enemy is constantly shifting.

But Rafa has been like a brother. It doesn't apply to him.

Antonio was my brother, too. He was also my father's son. He turned, didn't he? No one is beyond reproach.

I need to remember that.

"He's my family, Stefan."

"So am I. And I've been more family to you than he ever was."

"What do you want me to do? Cut off ties?"

"Thing is, I thought you already had."

"That was a long time ago. After your father died—"

"Was murdered."

"Was murdered, I wanted to have mine back. You can understand that, surely?"

"I can understand that, but what I don't understand is why I'm finding out through my fiancée. Why you asked her to lie to me about it."

"I didn't ask her to lie."

"Omission is a lie."

He opens his mouth, closes it and runs a hand through

his hair. "I knew you'd be pissed. She could have gotten hurt."

"She did. Two cars sideswiped you and you lied about that too."

"For the same reason. I lied for the same fucking reason."

"Who were they?"

"I don't know. I'd never seen them before. But one of them was at the house. In Pentedattilo."

I don't expect him to tell me that, but then again, he has more to gain than lose by offering me that small piece of information.

"And you don't know who he is?"

He shakes his head. "Or who he works for."

I finish my espresso and stand.

He stands too.

"I don't want you to lie to me again, Rafa. You know I consider you a brother."

"I know, Stefan. And I feel the same way about you. You are a brother to me."

We stand like that for a minute and I study him.

"We good?" he asks.

"Yeah. We're good." I check my watch.

"How is she?"

"She's okay. She's tough." I wonder how she's going to like what I have to tell her today. "Did you put anything other than the tracker on the new phone?" I ask. Rafa was the one who set up Gabriela's cell phone both times.

"Like what?" he asks. "Man, I'm starting to think she's right."

"Right about what?" I ask, noting the change of subject.

"She thinks you're jealous of me."

"Yeah, Gabriela likes to fuck with me." The word fuck and Gabriela in the same sentence make my cock stir.

"I just loaded the tracker on the phone like you wanted," he says. "I'm going to see Clara later, by the way," Rafa says. "Thought I'd go take her out before she loses her mind."

I chuckle. "She bored?" Clara likes to party and she and Rafa have a lot of fun together.

He rolls his eyes. "You'd think it was the end of the world."

"I can move her to Rome. She wanted to be closer by."

"I'll talk to her. Why don't you come with me? Like old times. I miss those days." It used to be the three of us having fun together, but I don't feel like it anymore.

"I've got too much going on here. Next time."

Rafa grins, one eye narrowing. "You like her."

"What?"

"Gabriela."

I just look at him.

"I saw how you looked at her at the well, Stefan. I'm not fucking blind. And if a woman looked at me the way she looks at you, hell, I'd stay home too."

"I don't know what you're talking about, Rafa."

"Just take care you don't like her too much. Makes her a weakness. You don't want to make a target out of her again. Your enemies will pounce when they see it."

I don't like his tone.

"Relax, man. I'm messing with you," he says when I don't reply.

I don't relax. "Tell Clara I said hello." I walk to the door.

"Will do. You alone?" he asks when I'm outside.

I nod.

"Don't do that, man. You know it's not safe."

"I'm just visiting my cousin. Why wouldn't I be safe?"

"There are eyes and ears everywhere. Just be fucking careful."

———

SOMETHING ABOUT ALL THAT BUGS ME THE WHOLE WAY HOME but when I get back and Millie tells me that one of my attorneys, Paulo Alessi, is here and waiting out on the patio, I put it out of my mind.

I walk out there to find him sitting with Gabriela. She's in a bikini, the little pink one. Too little.

He's laughing at something she says but stops and clears his throat nervously when he sees me. I move to stand behind her chair, putting both hands on her shoulders just to be sure everyone's clear where we stand and to whom she belongs.

"Stefan," he says, shifting his gaze quickly from Gabriela as he stands and extends his hand. "I got here early, and Gabriela was kind enough to keep me company."

I take a moment before I shake his hand. "I'm late. Thought I had more time. Ready to get started?"

"Of course," he says, picking up his briefcase.

"Nice to meet you, Paulo," Gabriela says, standing now that I've removed my hands from her shoulders. She extends her hand to him.

He looks at it, then at me, doing anything and everything to not appear to be looking at her in her too little bikini.

I give the briefest nod from behind her.

"Nice to meet you," he says with a quick shake of her hand.

"Millie," I call out as she's passing. "Show Paulo into my study."

"Of course," she says, and he follows her.

I look down at Gabriela's ass clad in a skimpy triangle of cloth and step closer to her to cup one cheek.

"I don't want you wearing these when I'm not around." I squeeze, inhale the scent of sunscreen at her neck. She smells like summer. Like sunshine.

She turns her face a little. "I thought you liked me sitting by the pool," she says, her tone seductive, like she knew what she was doing.

I give her ass a quick little smack that makes her jump.

"Hey."

"You're mine. You only wear these around me. Have Millie help you pick out some more modest suits."

She rolls her eyes. "You bought them for me, remember?"

"Put something else on until I'm finished and wait for me upstairs. Then I'll strip you naked and we'll get back to what we were doing earlier."

"Jealous much?" she mutters as she walks away.

I grab her ponytail and tug her backward. "Like getting your ass spanked much?"

"Maybe," she says, biting her lower lip as her eyes slide to my hand then back.

Fuck. Me.

I pull her to me to kiss her once, then bring my mouth to her ear. "When I'm finished, I'm going to bend you over my knee, bare your sweet little ass and spank you until you come."

Her breathing is short, and her eyes dark when she lifts her gaze to mine.

"Then I'm going to teach you how to suck my cock properly."

"Jesus."

"You go think about how you're going to look to me on

your knees with my cock stuffed down your throat after you've been spanked to orgasm. Think about how my come is going to taste when you swallow it."

I slide my free hand into the crotch of her skimpy bikini.

She makes a sound, something between a whimper and a moan, as she grinds herself against me.

"You dirty girl. You're already wet." I kiss her neck, her throat, then slide my hand out, smear it across her belly. "You like when I talk to you like this. Just make sure you don't put those fingers on your dirty little pussy and make yourself come until I can watch."

"You'll never know if I do," she says with a smirk.

"I'll know."

She reaches to touch my erection over my jeans. "Are you going to sport that hard-on through your meeting?"

I pull her hand away. "I'm a big boy. I'll manage my hard-on." I smack her ass again. "Now go to your room and wait for me."

12

GABRIELA

I slip a dress on over top of the bikini and decide to wait in the library instead of my room for Stefan to finish. I try reading but all I can do is think about what he said, what we're going to do.

And he's right that I want to slide my hand into my bikini bottoms and make myself come, but I somehow don't and for the next two hours, manage to get myself so worked up, I think I'm going to explode if he doesn't finish his meeting soon.

I leave the door open a crack so I can see when the attorney leaves. Miss Millie goes into the study with coffee at some point, but no one comes out.

When the doorbell rings an hour after that, I listen as Miss Millie lets whoever it is in.

"Mr. Sabbioni is expecting you," she says.

He's expecting someone else?

"Thank you," a male voice says.

I freeze.

I know this voice. It doesn't belong here. It's so out of place that it takes me a moment to make sense of who it is.

I get up, go to the door and peer through the crack.

"Right this way, Mr. Waverly," Miss Millie says.

I watch in shock as my father's most trusted attorney enters Stefan's study.

"What's he doing here?" I ask Miss Millie as soon as the study door is closed.

"Gabriela." She seems surprised to see me there. "I thought Stefan asked you to wait upstairs."

I guess he had but I hadn't realized it was an order. That he had a purpose in mind with his casual command. So casual I missed the command part.

"That's my father's attorney. What's he doing here?"

"I don't know, dear. Why don't you go upstairs and wait? I'm sure Stefan will explain once he's finished."

"I'm not going anywhere." My eyes are locked on the study door I'm marching toward.

"No, Gabriela." I see her signal to the soldier down the hall. "He won't like to be disturbed."

I manage to open the door just as that soldier takes hold of my arm.

"What the—" Stefan's gaze snaps to me. He's standing against the far wall, a pissed off expression on his face. The man I met earlier looks flustered and the only one smiling is Waverly.

"I'm sorry, Stefan," Miss Millie says, reaching to close the door as the soldier drags me backward.

"What's going on? Why is he here?" I ask, struggling to stand my ground, remembering what my father said about the modification to the contract. About how Stefan may not be so forthcoming about the change.

"I told you to wait in your room," Stefan says.

"Let me go!" I yell at the man holding me. "I have a right to know!"

"She does," Waverly says, a smug smile on his face.

I hate him. I hate that man. I always have. He helped my father cover up what he did to Gabe. He's always helped with the dirty work.

"Shut the fuck up, Waverly," Stefan tells him. "I'll tell her when it's time."

"Tell me now!"

"It's the modification your father mentioned, Gabriela," Waverly starts.

"Get her out of here!" Stefan orders and the soldier lifts me off my feet.

"Let go!"

"The one where you'll vow to never see or speak to your brother again."

What?

"You can understand it's far too dangerous now," he continues. "I mean, especially considering what happened to Mr. Roma—"

The door slams shut, and I'm carried up the stairs screaming and kicking.

He can't do this.

He can't.

Gabe is the last person I have left. He can't take him away too.

I struggle as the soldier enters my bedroom and drops me on my bed.

I scramble up, walk to the door, but he steps in front of it and folds his arms across his chest.

"Get out of my way!"

He just stands there like the stupid brick wall he is. I try to shove at him, try to move him, but it's impossible.

The balcony. I'll go through Stefan's room. But before

I'm even outside, the bedroom door opens and Stefan steps in. He orders the soldier out.

"Gabriela," he starts, tone calm.

I fly at him, a scream like a roar coming from my throat.

He catches me but I beat my fists against him, pound his chest until he takes hold of my wrists and forces them behind my back.

"I told you to wait here for a reason."

"So you could sneak Waverly in without my knowing? So you could make this change without my knowledge? How could you? After everything? How could you?"

He walks me backward, sits me on the edge of the bed. He keeps hold of my wrists as he leans down over me. "You don't understand, Gabriela—"

"Let me go. Don't touch me." I yell, struggling against him, ending up on my back for all the effort.

Stefan's on top of me, his weight almost too heavy. "There's a reason I waited."

"You waited." I squirm, my hands hurting with our combined weight on them. "How long have you known? Before my kidnapping? How long?"

He takes a deep breath in.

"You're hurting me. Let me go. Get off me."

"Calm down and I will."

"You want me to calm down?" I twist beneath him, pulling at my hands. It's useless until he decides to let me go, I know it. His grip is like an iron manacle. "You want me to calm down when my father's lawyer—that horrible man— tells me that I'll never see my brother again? Will never talk to him again? While you knew all along? While you *agreed*?"

"Christ," he says, letting go of my wrists and pushing off me to stand.

I stand too and without a moment's hesitation, I draw my arm back and I slap him so hard, his head jerks with the blow and the sound reverberates off the walls.

My hand stings as the room falls dead silent and when he turns his face back to mine, I see rage in his eyes. Pure and absolute rage.

"You are *never* to do that again," he says, speaking slowly, enunciating every word.

But that rage he's feeling? I can match it.

Hell, I can top it.

"No?" I ask, raising my arm again and swinging.

I don't make my target though. Stefan's no fool. He catches my wrist and throws me backward so hard that I bounce twice on the mattress.

He has one knee on the bed and closes his hand around my throat. "You don't fucking listen. That's your problem. You never fucking listen."

I claw at his forearm as he squeezes, digging out rivulets of skin and blood as I watch his crazed eyes darken. I slap at his arm, his chest. Anything.

He makes a sound, releases me.

"You're just like them! I hate you!" I scream, rolling onto my belly, scrambling away. I kick at him when he catches my ankle and drags me backward. His full weight is on me and one arm is locked around my neck, his bicep at my throat. When he flexes, I stop moving because I stop breathing.

"I don't want to hurt you, Gabriela," he says, his breath hot against my ear. "Don't make me hurt you."

A gurgling sound comes from my throat and he finally removes his arm.

"You'll hurt me anyway," I choke out the words.

He flips me over onto my back, keeps me trapped beneath him. "You don't understand—"

"I understand that you're no different than the man you hate."

His eyes narrow and I know those are the words he hates most. "You need to open your eyes and see the monsters for who they are."

"And the heroes for who they are?" I ask, sarcasm my poison.

But then Waverly's words ring through my ears again.

You'll vow to never see or speak to your brother again.

Sadness overwhelms me. I'm powerless. I always have been.

"You said you didn't want to hurt me."

This betrayal, it's harder to take, because I thought things were changing. I stupidly thought Stefan cared.

"Fuck." He lifts himself up a little and with his thumbs he wipes at my tears. "You said you wanted to trust me, Gabriela. Trust me."

When he told me I was sweet and innocent, what he meant was I'm a fool. A stupid, naïve fool and his perfect target. A perfect target for all of them.

"Are you even listening to me?" he asks.

"Get off me. Don't touch me."

Something in the way he looks at me changes and he slides off me. Stands. He looks down at me, runs a hand through his hair.

"I'm not going to hurt you. I never was. I told you that last night."

"I don't believe you." I pull myself up to a seat as far from him as possible, draw my knees up and wrap my arms around them.

I don't know what hurts worse, the fact that I'm going to lose my brother—because I will. My father, Stefan, men like them, you don't win against them, I know that.

But it's not that that's twisting my insides.

It's Stefan's betrayal.

I rest my forehead on my knees and close my eyes. My head hurts, and my heart hurts and I didn't think it was possible to feel any worse than I did in that well. Alone in that darkness and cold and stench. But it is.

"Gabriela—"

"Get out. Just get out."

His eyes narrow, jaw tightens. I know he wants to say something but I just bury my face again and I hear him walk to the door, open it. "She's not to leave this room until I send for her," he says to the man outside.

I wasn't going to leave. Where would I go?

The door closes.

I just sit there, and I feel more alone than I've ever felt in my life.

13

STEFAN

B y the time I get downstairs, the paperwork's been updated. I sign and, fuck, what I'd give to punch the stupid grin off Waverly's face. To slam my fist into it and knock out his over-bleached teeth.

But I force my hands into my pockets, fisting them there, thinking about her upstairs.

Doesn't she know me by now? At least a little?

"Mr. Marchese will be in touch," Waverly says.

"Mr. Marchese can go fuck himself," I reply, never taking my eyes off him.

He closes his briefcase, gathers it up and is smart enough not to extend his hand for me to shake.

"I'll see myself out," he says.

Like hell he will. One of my men accompanies him to his car and follows him out the gate. I pour myself a whiskey.

Over the next thirty minutes, Paulo prepares another form, one Waverly and Marchese won't see until it's too late. He straightens, smiles awkwardly as if he didn't just witness what happened.

A single heroic act does not a hero make.

No. No hero here.

I run a hand through my hair, unable to get the way she looked at me out of my head.

"Finished?" I snap.

"Yes, it's finished. She just needs to sign this. I'll pick it up and file it once everything is in order."

Once we're man and wife. And then only after I've greased many palms.

"Thank you," I force.

"You're welcome. I'll be heading home, then. Let me know if you need anything else."

I nod, shake his hand and when he's gone, I close my office door and study the papers.

How will she feel about this? Will she see it as a heroic act or a heinous one?

I know the real answer. I know myself.

I tell one of the guards to bring her downstairs and get up to switch on the stereo. Mephistopheles sings, brokering Faust's deal with the devil. Fitting.

Gabriela walks into the study not five minutes later. Or, more accurately, she's walked inside. And what I see in her eyes is betrayal. Hopelessness. And hate. And all I can think is she's too young and too innocent for this.

To know so much despair.

But she is who she is. The devil's daughter. And I just brokered my own deal.

I've stolen her.

And I'm not finished yet.

"Sit down, Gabriela."

She folds her arms across her chest and shakes her head, eyes accusing as she presses her back to the wall.

"I said sit." I think about last night. About this morning. Hell, about a few hours ago at the pool. That girl is gone.

This one, she's the one from before. The one who was hauled into her father's study to sign away her life.

"Fuck you, Stefan. You're a liar."

I study her, take in the words. Feel her hate.

"Sit down before I make you."

She swallows. She knows I will.

Her hands are fists as she walks toward the couch and perches on the very edge.

"After everything, you trust me so little?" I ask.

"You lie constantly. You play games with me."

"I haven't lied to you. I've been fairly straight forward, in fact."

She snorts, shakes her head. "Really? Sneaking my father's attorney here while I wait for you upstairs. While I wait for you to *fuck me* upstairs, that's straightforward?"

"This is my house. I wasn't sneaking anyone in. I needed to get this done before I could tell you what—"

"Save it." She's on her feet, hands at her sides. "Tell it to someone who cares. Who gives a fuck what you say. Every single word that comes out of your mouth is a fucking lie."

My hands are fisted too and I'm trying to be patient. To see from her point of view. She's young. A girl. And she's emotional as fuck. Marchese is trying to drive a wedge between us. I know it. Doesn't she see it? What's happening between us now, it's exactly what he wants.

And I realize something.

I don't want to lose her.

But fuck, my patience is running thin.

"My eyes are open now," she continues. "See, where you get me wrong is that you think I need to choose between you and my father. That I need to make one of you the angel so the other can be the monster. I don't. Because there are two monsters in this doomed fairy tale." She takes a breath.

"You're right about one thing, though. A single heroic act does not a hero make. A hundred wouldn't make you a hero, Stefan, because you aren't that. You will never be that."

She turns on her heel and almost makes it a full step away before I catch her by her hair. She fights me when I spin her around and march her to my desk.

"Your eyes are far from open. And this thing, Gabriela, this thing between us, it's no fairy tale." I push her over the desk. I hold her face about two inches from the piece of paper there. "Read."

"Let me go."

"I said read."

"I'm not interested—"

I haul her up, get in her face. "Do you *need* me to lock you up in a tower, *princess*?" I spit. "Is that it? Because you *need* me to be your monster? Is that the only way you know how to deal with men? Are we all monsters?"

I watch her eyes water but I don't let go.

"You've proven yourself over and over again," she says, still fighting even though she knows she's lost.

"Read," I say, turning her face back to the desk

"Let go of my hair! You're hurting me!"

"But isn't that what monsters do? Fucking read. Get all the fucking facts before you cast stones and once you have them, I may allow you to beg for my forgiveness. Of course, you'll have to do it on your knees."

"I will never kneel to you."

I chuckle. "Before the night is out. Read."

She pushes against the desk to raise herself up, but I keep her down over it and smack her ass hard. She grunts, reaching back to cover the spot.

"Read."

"I don't want to!"

"That's too bad. You had some leeway with me but that's finished. Don't push me now. I'm very close to losing my temper with you. Fucking read."

I only release her when she moves the sheet of paper a little, and I know she's reading.

She flips one page, then another. It's a few minutes before she turns to me, eyebrows knitted together.

"You can't do this," she says, straightening. "My brother isn't a part of this."

"Your father made him a part of it."

"You can't—"

"I can. And you'll sign. Because it's the only way to save him."

"No."

"Think, Gabriela."

She looks away, her forehead furrowing as she thinks hard. She shakes her head, opens her mouth but she's like a broken record. "You can't."

"You compare me to your father, yet you tell me you want to trust me, but you know what I think? I think you're full of shit. I think you need to be locked away in that tower you've built for yourself because that's the only way you know how to survive."

"He can't be a part of this."

"This agreement will save your brother. It will save you both."

She stares up at me and I can see her battle to make sense of what she's seen. "It will deliver him to you," she says.

I force a deep inhale, count to ten. "And what exactly do you think I'll do with him?"

"I think you won't only bury my father, but you'll bury my brother and me along with him."

My hands fist. "You believe that? Still?"

"Punish me if you have to but leave my brother out of it."

"What would you have me do? Put cigarettes out on your back? Cut you? Is that the same deal you made with your father? Let him hurt you to save your brother?"

"That's not...My brother...he's already lost so much." I see in her face she knows this is going to happen. And her pain, it twists something inside me.

"I don't do this to hurt you," I say, cupping her face. "Can't you believe that?"

"But you do hurt me."

"Only because you refuse to see." I smear a tear across her cheek. "You're a sad little thing and I don't want you sad. Don't you understand?"

"Then change it. Take your name off it."

"I can't do that."

"Because you don't trust me and yet you expect me to trust you. I'll do whatever you want, Stefan. I will."

"I know you will."

"Please just change it. Take your name off it."

With my hand at the back of her head, I pull her to me and lean down to kiss her forehead, keeping my lips there for a long moment. I then kiss her temple, move to her ear.

"He'll do anything to take you from me. He'll do anything to get you back. He thinks I'll give you up when he pulls his little trick—"

"What trick?"

"But he doesn't know about us. He couldn't understand. You'll sign the papers. Tomorrow. After we're married. And you'll have your brother back."

"And we'll both be at your mercy."

"Am I so terrible?" I step backward, away from her.

"Have I mistreated you, Gabriela? What have I done but try to make you happy?"

"Happy? So this is you trying to make me happy? You're deluded."

My jaw tightens. "You want your brother. I'm getting him for you."

"By taking guardianship of him yourself!"

"It's the only way."

"Liar!" she screams, slapping both hands against my chest and trying to shove me away.

"Gabriela." I catch her wrists, pull them off me and the moment I do, she spits at me.

I turn my face away in time and from the look in hers, I get the feeling she's more surprised than I am by the act.

For a long moment, we stand like that, staring at one another, tension so thick between us that it's hard to breathe.

"You learn nothing." Rage burns me from the inside, coming to a boil. "Go to your room," I order through gritted teeth.

"I won't sign."

"You will. Now go."

"I hate you. I will always hate you."

I swallow, squeeze her wrists, fury churning inside my gut. "I'm warning you to go. Now. Before it's too late."

"It's already too late."

"You know what?" I exhaled, shake my head. "You're right."

14

GABRIELA

I see the switch flip inside him. It's the strangest thing. The scariest thing.

Because just like that, he's the man from that first night again. The crazed one.

There's a single moment where time feels like it's suspended over us. Where it's like we're both locked in place, and the instant I gain control of my legs, the instant I tell them to move, to run, to carry me away from this monster, he tugs me so hard, I bounce off his chest and I'd fall if he didn't have me.

He walks me backward to the wall, pushes me roughly against it. Holds me there.

Music swells, opera, a soprano. Marguerite, I think. It's Faust and Marguerite.

They're doomed. They were from the start.

I watch Stefan unbuckle his belt as he mutters under his breath. His eyes are fierce, dark, and hard and burning.

With a swoosh, he tugs the belt free and the sound, it fills me with fear.

"Tomorrow," he says, doubling the belt in his hand,

taking the buckle in his palm. He takes both of my wrists into one of his hands and stretches my arms over my head. My dress rises, exposing my thighs.

He raises the belt.

"Stefan don't!"

He brings it down across the fronts of my legs and I'm shocked by the sudden, searing pain. Silenced by it.

"Tomorrow, you'll marry me." He brings it down again and this time, I do scream, and I realize how dark it is in here. How loud the music is. Was it this loud when we were screaming at each other?

The scene reaches its crescendo.

The execution is coming. Marguerite will be beheaded soon.

"You'll wear what I tell you to wear and you'll smile and look pretty, and you'll do exactly as you're told. And if you don't, I will strip you naked and lash you from the tops of your shoulders down to your ankles."

Another lash and another and another. My thighs are on fire.

"Please! God. Please stop. It hurts!"

"And once we're man and wife, you'll sign the petition for guardianship. Am I clear?" he asks, punctuating with another stroke.

"It hurts!" I'm crying. Sobbing. Fuck.

He lashes me again, three more strokes before gripping my jaw in his belt hand, fingers digging into me. "Those won't scar," he says, his face so close to mine our noses are touching. "I'm sure your father would do much worse. Now do you understand, or do you need me to whip you properly?"

"I hate you," I manage.

"I don't care."

"I will always hate you." My throat closes up as hot tears streak my cheeks.

He forces me to my knees, keeps me down there. I guess he's making good on his threat of earlier.

"You sound like a broken record. This is bigger than your hate. Now answer my question. More strokes or do you understand?"

He watches me and I see the blur of him through my tear-filled eyes. "I understand," I spit. Because what choice do I have?

He nods and the belt clangs to the floor beside me. When he releases me, I sag backward. I guess it's good I'm already on the floor. My legs wouldn't hold me upright. I look down at the exposed part of my thighs. See the thick, angry red welts on them.

Stefan looks at me for a moment longer, but I can't read his eyes and my brain, my stupid brain, goes to the other night. To how he was on Skull Rock. How he talked to me. How he held me. How he kissed me.

I watch him turn, watch him walk away. Pour himself a drink.

With the heel of one hand, I wipe my eyes as he looks back at me down on my knees. He swallows the contents of his glass. And when he stalks toward me, I press my back against the wall, as if I could disappear into it.

He ignores my whimper but leans down to cup my chin and he's almost gentle when he tilts my face up to his and I watch him watch me for a long moment.

"You're a sad little thing," he says.

And I think he's never been more right.

15
___

GABRIELA

The papers I'm to sign are a petition for Gabe's guardianship. And it would be a good thing. But there's a catch. There's always a catch.

How long has Stefan planned on taking guardianship of my brother? While he was lying on that beach with me? While he was kissing me?

A knock on my door interrupts my thoughts.

"Are you ready?" Miss Millie asks, peering her head into my room.

Does she know what happened last night? Does she know I don't want this? That I'm being forced to do this?

I shift my gaze back to my reflection. I don't look like I did the night of the engagement party. Not elegant and sophisticated. I'm wearing minimal make-up. Just some cover up, mascara and lip gloss. My face is pale, and I can't hide the puffy redness from all the crying.

My hair falls loose to my shoulders, the bangs tucked behind my ear. I'm not wearing the pretty hat that comes with the dress Stefan chose but I am dressed. It was delivered this morning, my replacement wedding dress. And with it came a note:

Remember what will happen if you make me come up there to dress you.

S

No 'x' this time.

And I am dressed.

At least it's not the hideous gown.

"Ready," I say, standing, the skin of my thighs tight, a painful reminder of last night's whipping. A taste of what will happen if I disobey.

No women to prepare me today. No need. Today is a decoy. A means to an end. Just like I am a means to an end. If I was forgetting that, he reminded me of it last night.

"You look beautiful," Miss Millie says.

I don't want to look beautiful.

I'm wearing a white lace off-the-shoulder dress that comes to my knees. Black would have been more fitting. A thick satin belt cinches my waist and the sleeves come to my elbows. A pair of high satin heels finishes the look.

It's simple, I guess. At least compared to the other one.

Miss Millie is wearing a pretty navy-blue suit and for the first time since I've known her, makeup.

"Stefan is waiting downstairs," she says and opens the door wider.

I nod, glance back at my reflection but I don't recognize myself.

What a sham this is. What a sham my life has become.

I straighten my spine and walk out of the bedroom. I can see him waiting with Rafa in the foyer and they both look up at me. Stefan's face doesn't change. I don't know if Rafa's does because I'm only looking at Stefan.

Stefan.

Satan.

Stefan.

He's beautiful, just like all fallen angels are. I thought so even that first night. The night he smelled of death. The night he risked death sneaking into my bedroom on my sixteenth birthday to give me that gift. To make me that promise that he would be back for me. That he would steal me away.

He's dressed in a dark suit with a dark shirt and tie and never takes his eyes off me as I walk down the stairs, remembering last night, remembering his warning. The welts on my thighs burn but it's good. The pain won't let me forget what he is. What he's capable of.

I am a means to an end. That reality was muddled a few nights ago, but now, it's crystal clear.

I'll marry Stefan Sabbioni today. Weeks earlier than planned.

And then we'll petition for guardianship of my brother. Take him out of my father's hands so he can't use him as a pawn. Put him in Stefan's hands instead.

And there's that catch. Stefan will become his guardian. Not me.

Out of the frying pan and into the fire.

There I go again.

I didn't think I'd be taking my brother with me.

"You look beautiful, Gabriela," Stefan says, closing his hands softly around my wrists, his cheek brushing mine as he brings his mouth to my ear to whisper his question to me. "Are you going to behave?"

His body is just touching mine and he's moved our arms

so his are bent around me, the position just enough to denote possession.

"Last night's warning stands," he adds when I don't answer right away.

"You mean last night's threat?" I ask.

He grins, tightens his hold on me until I wince.

"Your answer?"

"I have no choice. You didn't leave me with one. My brother's well-being is at stake, Stefan, so don't worry, I'll do as I'm told."

Does he feel my hate? Does it roll off me in icy waves because that's what I feel like now. Ice. But maybe that's not hate. Maybe that's betrayal.

Stefan shifts his grip to my hand and walks me toward the door. Rafa and Miss Millie follow and a few minutes later, we're loaded into the SUVs and our motorcade is driving into Palermo proper.

It's surreal, this.

I look at my husband to be. He's texting something into his phone.

Why does it matter if I'm married to him or not? Why does it matter if it's now or two weeks from now? I'm his. I can be his prisoner and his wife. I am already the former. Because no matter what, he won't let me go. And this, once we file those papers and he gains guardianship of my brother, it's one more thing he'll have to bind me to him.

What happens when he gets everything he wants?

What happens to Gabe? To me?

We arrive at City Hall in Palermo. It's beautiful. Just what you'd expect in an Italian city with its ancient architecture, the fountains and sculptures outside, the tourists. The never-ending crowds of tourists.

The area that's been cordoned off is opened to us and

our motorcade passes through. We pull to a stop at an entrance blocked to tourists. I wonder if they rolled the red carpet out for us especially when Stefan comes to help me out. When he wraps his arm around my back and when I can't move, he nudges me along.

This is happening. I know it. I don't know why I'm dragging my feet.

A man comes to greet Stefan. He has his own entourage. I'm introduced to him. He's the mayor. And the woman beside him is his wife. They brought their kids to the wedding.

I shake hands, smile, but it all feels strange. Like I'm standing in a bubble while they're all here around me. While they're living this day and I'm displaced. Out of time. A ghost.

"Gabriela?" Stefan asks, eyebrows raised, a warning in his eyes.

I blink, look around and realize they're all watching me, waiting for something.

"I'm sorry. What?"

"Are you ready?" Stefan asks me.

I look at him. At them. I touch my forehead. It's clammy even though I'm shuddering with cold. Sweat comes away and I feel lightheaded.

"Let's get her out of the sun," someone says and as if to prove some point, my knees give out and there's a joint swelling of gasps as Stefan catches me before I fall.

He's angry. I see it. He holds me close to him and I reach up to touch his arm, his chest. I want to push him away, but to those watching, it must look like a lover's touch.

"It's the heat," someone says. "She's too warm."

Stefan cups my face to make me look at him. His eyes

convey their warning. He leans in close and stubble tickles my ear. "Stand up."

He pulls back and I nod. What can I do?

I stand but I'm unsteady.

Everyone walks into the air-conditioned building and I feel better. Maybe it was the heat. At least in part.

"Sit down here, dear," Miss Millie says, and she takes the glass of water from one of the men and hands it to me.

I take it and sip. "I'm okay," I tell her as I watch Stefan watching me even as he talks to the mayor.

I think about my mom and realize I've forgotten more of her face. I think about something else too. About memories vanishing. And I'm wrong. Only the good ones vanish. The bad ones, we live them over and over again in our minds.

I wish I could forget how she died and remember how she lived. I miss her so much, it hurts, and I let myself daydream for just a second about how things might have been if she'd lived. If he hadn't killed her. Would my father be a different person? Would he have done what he did to Stefan's family? Would Stefan be a stranger to me?

And what about Gabe? Would he be himself?

There's a commotion and I realize, once again, that I was distracted. Stefan's hazel eyes are still on me, though.

He says something to one of the men and a few minutes later, the room is cleared. He comes to sit beside me.

"Bad luck," I say.

"What?" he asks, sliding his hand under my dress to rest it on my thigh. He traces one of the welts. Is this a reminder?

"To see the bride before the ceremony," I say.

He just studies me. "All the luck I've ever had has been bad."

"Maybe that's because you're bad."

"Maybe. Are you ready?"

"No."

"What's the difference between now or a few weeks from now? You were always going to be mine, Gabriela. This was always going to happen."

"I want an agreement between us. I want just this one thing."

His jaw tightens.

"My brother. Put me down as his legal guardian. You can do whatever you want to me and I'll do what you say, but you leave him alone. No contact. No nothing."

"Will that make you happy?"

"I don't think you care about my happiness. You don't have to pretend you do. I see you for what you are now, and I won't forget again."

He shifts his gaze away and for one moment, I see something that doesn't fit. Doesn't belong. A flicker of something almost painful.

When he returns his gaze to mine, it's gone. "You used to see a different me."

"I was wrong." It hurts to say the words.

It takes him a moment, but he stands, holds out his hand. "Come."

"Do you agree?"

"You know I can't do that. Now don't make this harder than it has to be. My intention is not to take him from you. The opposite. It was always to give him to you. Think of it as a wedding gift."

"A wedding gift?" I can't believe him.

Before I can say more, he takes hold of my arm and lifts me to my feet.

"Our guests are waiting."

16
———

STEFAN

The wedding ceremony, as fraudulent as it feels, is legally binding.

The small room is pretty enough, with high ceilings and large windows. Blue drapes with little yellow flowers on them match the carpet and the upholstery of the chairs situated to face the large antique table at the front.

It's all old and a little dusty but it will serve its purpose.

Gabriela doesn't walk down the aisle toward me. I walk her, her arm tucked into mine, the small bouquet of flowers something someone must have handed her on her way in because I've never seen them before. She holds them absently, her eyes locked on the front of the room.

It's like she's not here.

Like she's blocking this out.

At least she's not crying. Not fighting. She won't, though. There's too much at stake.

If she doesn't do this, she will lose her brother.

If she does, she'll gain guardianship of him. Well, I will, technically but I don't have any interest in Gabe Marchese apart from using him to screw his father especially when he thought he'd screw me in the process.

He cut Gabriela out of the will entirely. Reverted to the old family rule of inheritance to the first-born. She doesn't know this yet. If she did, she'd only accuse me of taking guardianship of her brother for the inheritance, and she'd be right. But that's not solely my reason. I meant it when I said I didn't want her to be sad.

Did Marchese think I'd give her back when he changed the will? That I'd call it quits and tuck tail? No. He's too clever to believe that.

But when it comes to Gabriela, Gabriel Marchese is odd. He lets his emotions get in the way of his thinking. No, not emotions, exactly. How he is with her is strange, to say the least. It's more possession than fatherly love that rules him.

And I don't think that possession has anything to do with me.

The memory of how he looked at her at our engagement party returns and I find myself tugging her a little closer.

She turns to look at me.

Sad little thing.

Collateral damage. Remember Antonio. Remember your father. Remember why you're doing this.

We reach the front of the room and stand before the mayor who will be the officiant of this sham marriage. Rafa stands at my side and Millie at hers. The only other guests are a handful of soldiers and the mayor's family.

Gabriela doesn't deserve what she's getting. I know it. I've known it from day one. But she is choosing how this goes. I mean it when I say I don't want to be her enemy, but she makes it impossible.

Collateral damage.

The mayor signals for the few witnesses to sit down and

he begins the ceremony. Gabriela answers for her part with little nudging from me and I wonder if anyone's noticed she understands the Italian just fine, only she answers in English.

When the time comes for the rings, Rafa takes two out of his pocket and hands them to me.

I take Gabriela's hand and repeat the mayor's words as I slide the ring—a wide platinum band that matches her engagement ring—onto her already crowded finger.

She looks down at it as I do it. Down at our two hands. Mine big, hers so small, so delicate, it disappears inside my palm.

I can crush her. It wouldn't take much.

When it's her turn to place the ring on my finger, she meekly takes the ring I offer her, a matching band of platinum, and repeats the mayor's words, pledging her obedience to me, as she slides it onto my finger.

She doesn't look at me once.

And when we're pronounced husband and wife and the ceremony is over, I pull her to me and kiss her, a chaste kiss on her pretty, resistant mouth.

One of the mayor's staff enters the room carrying a tray filled with glasses of champagne for each of us. His wife and family are oblivious to Gabriela's mood, her mental absence. The mayor isn't, but that doesn't matter. I pay him enough and he'll do what he's told. If I brought her here in chains, kicking and screaming, he'd still do what he was told and marry us.

Once the champagne is drunk and everyone has kissed Gabriela's cheeks and offered us their congratulations, we're left alone in the room with the mayor. Two soldiers stand outside and Rafa and Millie are on their way to the restaurant for our small reception.

"Just a few signatures and you can be on your way," the mayor says.

This one is the certificate of marriage. I'll make sure her father has a copy before the end of the day.

I watch Gabriela and wonder if she hears anything at all as she takes the pen offered to her. She glances to me and I nod once. She looks back at the certificate on the desk and, a moment later, she signs.

I doubt the next signature I'll need from her back at the house will be given as easily.

When she's finished, I take the pen and sign my name and it's done.

Gabriela is my wife.

I set the pen on the desk and turn to her. She's looking up at me, her expression that of someone beaten.

"Congratulations, once again," the mayor says, standing, extending his hand to me.

I shake it, thank him.

Gabriela, too, shakes his hand, and we're on our way to the reception.

"I'm tired," Gabriela complains when we're in the car. "Do we have to do this?"

"Are you in a hurry to get home?"

"Your house is not my home."

"You called it that a few days ago."

"You were a different man a few days ago."

"Same man. Same intentions."

"That's right. Bury all things Marchese."

I lean toward her, lift her chin with one finger. "It's a good thing you're not a Marchese anymore then."

She tugs her head away and watches out the window for the twenty-minute ride.

The small restaurant is set just for our party with tables

decorated formally, everything white, flowers, tablecloths,
napkins. Champagne corks are popped, and my wife takes
her flute when I hand it to her, and she swallows the
contents.

"What are you doing?" I ask her when she holds the
empty glass out to me.

"Celebrating." When I don't take her glass, she stops a
waiter who is passing and swaps her empty glass out for a
full one.

"Take care, sweetheart," I tell her as she downs her
second glass.

"Stefan," it's Rafa.

I turn away from my bride. "Yes?"

"My father's here. Had some trouble on the road. Flat
tire."

"Did he?"

As a sign of good will, I invited Rafa's father. He's
brought Clara with him and is followed in by a man
carrying a large gift covered in white silk cloth.

I glance at Gabriela as he approaches. For as well as she
guards her features, I see recognition flit across her face
when she sees him.

He smiles. "Stefan," he says, dragging his gaze to mine.
"Congratulations." He leans in to hug me, patting my back.

"Thank you, Uncle," I say.

He turns to Gabriela and smiles wide. I study him for a
moment, watch the way he looks at her. See from the corner
of my eye the way Rafa shifts his gaze between his father
and Clara.

"Gabriela, this is Francesco Catalano. My uncle and
Rafa's father."

He holds his hand out to her.

She looks at it, then turns to me. I wonder if it's the

missing finger that upsets her, but she collects herself and smiles, slides her hand into his and this gesture, this placing of her small, vulnerable hand inside his older, butchered one, it makes my hackles go up.

"You make a beautiful bride," he says, raising her hand to his lips. "Congratulations, my dear."

"Thank you," she manages, her voice a whisper.

"I have a gift for the bride," he says, giving me an apologetic look.

I smile. I don't care about gifts. But I am curious about his.

He gestures to the man carrying the large, covered thing and the man brings it over, sets it on the table near us.

We all turn to it as Francesco tugs the silk covering off and someone gasps at the sudden commotion of flapping wings.

Two small birds in a cage. A golden cage. Unique. Specially made, I know from looking at it.

"It's a replica of Stefan's house," my uncle tells her as she steps toward it. She touches the golden door, peers down through it to the birds. "Pure gold. And almost as beautiful as the bride."

"Birds?"

"Lovebirds for the lovebirds," my uncle says.

My hands fist.

"They're so pretty," Gabriela says, smiling, leaning down to put a finger inside the cage, petting one of the birds who comes close to it.

"Not yet named. You'll have to do that."

He watches her, and I shift my gaze from the cage, to her, to him. I don't care about the birds.

She looks up at him. "It's beautiful," she finally says. "And fitting."

My nails dig into the palms of my hands.

Francesco smiles. "You haven't seen the best part," he says. He opens the small door and I can see the workmanship is top notch. He reaches inside to push on the floor of the cage. When he does, a trap door of sorts opens.

Gabriela peers close. "What is it?"

"This may be more for my nephew," he says, giving me a proud look over his shoulder.

No. Not proud.

Calculated.

He pushes a button and music begins to play. A familiar scene.

Gabriela's mouth opens and she turns to me but I'm so angry, all I see is red.

"Faust. Your favorite opera, I believe?" he asks.

It's the scene we heard last night as our own tragedy played out.

"It's perfect," Gabriela says. She puts her hands on his arms and leans in to plant a soft kiss on his cheek. "Thank you very much, Mr. Catalano."

"Let's eat!" Rafa calls out from somewhere behind me as music starts to play and people move to their tables.

17

GABRIELA

I'm sent to my room to await my husband's summons. At least Rafa carried my wedding gift upstairs. It's heavier than I expected but the birds are sweet.

I recognized the man introduced to me as Rafa's father as the man Rafa had met with that day in Taormina. I know it from the way he walked. As slimy as he seems to me, I can see he gets under Stefan's skin and that alone brings a smile to my face. Albeit a bitter one.

Thinking back to a few days ago, hell, even yesterday morning, how are we here now? How do I feel about my husband? I've seen the gentle side. The caring side. This one, though, the one from last night, from today, he's the ruthless one.

I endured the afternoon in that restaurant. I sat beside my husband and sipped my champagne, probably more than I should have, and ate my food, probably too little in proportion to the champagne, and somehow, I survived it. And now we're back at the Palermo house and I'm waiting for Stefan in my room as I study the gift his uncle gave me.

Stefan didn't like it and I understand.

The cage—it's my cage. This house, my prison.

Two birds. He and I. We're both prisoners in a way, aren't we? He to his hate. Me to him.

But lovebirds we are not.

The music, that particular scene. Ironic that it's the same scene that played last night as we battled. As I learned what Stefan would do.

I open the little door and push the button to play the music again. From his question to Stefan I know it wasn't an accidental choice of music, although not the most fitting gift for a wedding. Well, a true wedding with two people who love each other. Maybe it is fitting for ours.

My phone buzzes with a text message, interrupting my thoughts. It's on the nightstand charging.

I pick it up. The name of the sender doesn't register, but I know the number. It's my father. How did he even get this number? And does he know what's happened? That Stefan and I are married?

I click into the message which was sent an hour ago but because my phone was out of charge, I only see it now. I read it, thinking how unlike my father to send me a text.

I hear congratulations are in order. For the best, I suppose. I don't think I could have handed you over to the Sicilian bastard in a proper church. I hope you enjoy my gift. It was quite an extravagance, all that gold, the workmanship.
Know that nothing I do is to harm you. It is all to destroy him and save you. I hope you will enjoy all the surprises of your gilded cage.
Daddy

Daddy.

The word turns my stomach.

Daddy is reserved for fathers who love their daughters. Not for men like my father.

I re-read the message.

I hope you will enjoy all the surprises of your gilded cage.

But Rafa's father gave me this gift, didn't he?

I get up, go to it, study it more closely when a knock on my door startles me.

"Yes?"

It's not Stefan, I know. He wouldn't have knocked.

The door opens and Rafa is standing out in the hallway. His gaze slides from me to the cage and back but if he knows anything about it, he keeps it hidden from me.

"Congratulations, Gabriela. I didn't get a chance to tell you that," he says, coming into my bedroom and closing the door behind him.

"You know it's not real."

He studies me for a long moment. "You like the gift?" he asks, eyes steady.

Am I reading into his gaze? Does he know something about it or is he making small talk?

"It's beautiful but extravagant. Your father doesn't even know me," I test.

Rafa smiles and it's that same smile from the first time when he took me jogging. "He's trying to get back into Stefan's good graces."

Small talk. I don't need small talk.

"Why was the same man who sideswiped us at that house, Rafa?"

He never shifts his gaze away. "I'm trying to figure that out too," he says, his forehead creasing. Is it in concern?

"You were angry after your meeting with your father."

"I was. But I'm often angry after meeting with my father." He walks around me to the cage. He runs a hand over the golden bars. "It's nice." He turns to me. "You should come downstairs and say goodbye. Stefan will expect it."

Anxiety fills my belly. "He wants me to sign a petition to get guardianship of my brother."

"Better for your brother, isn't it?"

"Becoming Stefan's pawn rather than my father's? How is that better? It's just different."

"It was your father who put him in Clear Meadows to begin with."

"How do you know that?"

He studies me, then makes a point of checking his watch. "I have to take Clara home. Let me walk you downstairs."

"I can find my own way."

He walks to the door and opens it. "I'll escort you."

Stefan's words come back to me. *There's nothing nice about Rafa.*

"Just a minute," I say, "I need to use the bathroom."

He nods, gestures for me to go ahead. He doesn't leave the room.

I walk into the bathroom and close the door. Standing in front of the mirror, I run the cold water and splash a handful on my face, then dry it.

What did Stefan say about allies and enemies and that constantly shifting line? Rafa is not my friend. I know that. I've known it all along. I guess the real question is how passive or active an enemy is he to me?

I feel like I'm locked in a cage and in each corner is another monster.

"Gabriela," Rafa asks with a soft knock.

"Coming," I say, wondering which of the monsters will bury me.

18

GABRIELA

The house is dark but for the light that pours from Stefan's study. I hear Clara's familiar, irritating laughter and almost stop as my hands fist. I wonder if Rafa notices this shift in me. I think he might because it's then that he puts his hand at my lower back. I hurry my step until he's not touching me and I'm standing just inside the study.

"I didn't realize we still had guests," I say, my eyes on Clara.

She finishes her champagne and I hate that she looks so perfect. That she's wearing white. Isn't it in poor taste to wear white to a wedding that's not your own?

Why do you care?

Stefan and Clara both stand.

Clara looks me over as she walks toward me. I smell her perfume when she leans to kiss my cheek, or more accurately, to touch her icy cheek to mine.

"Congratulations," she says to me, drawing back. "Welcome to the family."

Family. Christ. Who's worse, the Marchese's or the Sabbioni's? We take dysfunction to a whole other level.

"Ready to go, Clara?" Rafa asks.

She goes to Rafa, stands a little closer than what I'd think is normal for cousins but I'm apparently the only one who notices the oddity.

"See you tomorrow, Stef," Rafa says as he gestures for Clara to walk out ahead of him.

"See you then," Stefan says and a moment later, he closes the door and turns to face me.

"Are they together?" I ask.

"They're cousins."

"But are they together?"

Stefan shrugs, walks behind his desk to take out a folder. "They fuck now and again, if that's what you're asking."

"Did the three of you..." I start but stop as soon as I hear my own words.

Stefan's eyes gleam and he gives me a one-sided grin. "For all your inexperience you have a dirty mind."

I steel my spine. "You all seem so cozy. Always have."

"Clara likes to have fun."

He doesn't deny it. I wish he did. Wish he'd tell me I was crazy.

"You're my wife, Gabriela."

"Don't worry, I don't ask out of jealousy, just curiosity. You can fuck whoever you like."

He comes around the desk, his walk that of a predator. He doesn't waste words or give me any space, but one hand fists my hair and he walks me backward until I'm at the wall.

"Be very careful."

"I'm just telling you it's okay. Isn't that what you want?"

His gaze skims my face, hovering for a moment at my mouth before returning to my eyes. "So you're giving me your *permission*?" He shakes his head, snorts. "Are you expecting the same allowance from me?"

"I don't need your *allowance*."

His fist tightens and I lean my head backward a little, trying to alleviate the pain.

"This is a sham. You and I both know it," I say.

He studies me for a long moment but then abruptly releases me and steps backward. "The papers are ready."

Yes. The papers. The reason for this whole thing.

I glance to his desk, to the stack of pages awaiting my signature. "You'll take me to see him?"

He nods.

"Do you promise?"

"I promise."

I don't have a choice. Well, I do. I can leave him in my father's care and never see him again.

I walk over to the desk, pick up the pen, sign my name and it's done. Stefan's petition is ready.

"My father doesn't know, does he?" I ask.

"Not yet." He looks over the papers, then turns his gaze to me. "You did the right thing."

"I guess we'll find out."

"It's late."

Anxiety fills my belly. I know what comes next.

"Let's go upstairs," he says.

"I don't love you," I say, the words abrupt and out of place.

He cocks his head to the side. "Love has nothing to do with this. You told me so yourself."

"We don't have to do this part. We—"

"This marriage will be consummated. Tonight."

A chill runs along my spine and I close one hand over the opposite arm.

Stefan puts a hand at my lower back. "Let's go, Gabriela."

Will he make me if I say no?

"Don't make this harder than it needs to be," he says, as if reading my mind. "Upstairs." I feel the pressure of his hand and my legs are somehow moving, somehow carrying me out of the study, to the stairs and up to his room.

My heart races, goosebumps cover my flesh.

This isn't how I want my first time. Or any time.

He closes the door behind us, and I step away, look at the bed. I've slept in it. Been naked in it. Been naked in it with him.

This, though, tonight, like this, it's different.

He comes to me and I back away. I can't help it and it's not a conscious choice, but I only stop when I run out of space.

I put my hands up against his chest.

He takes my hands, draws my arms upward, taking both wrists in one hand using the other to tilt my face up to his. His touch is different than I expect. Gentler. And I can't seem to find my voice.

"You're beautiful. I thought so from the first time I saw you."

My body seems to be vibrating, every nerve ending alive with anxiety and anticipation and something else. Something I don't want to acknowledge.

"I was sixteen," I manage.

"And already beautiful. I won't hurt you, Gabriela."

"You will, Stefan."

He studies me, thoughtful. Then his free hand moves to unzip the back of my dress and I guess it's happening. It's happening now. Like this.

I didn't think it'd be like this.

But fuck him. I will not cry. I will not let him see weakness. I will not let him see fear.

He releases my wrists, tugs the dress off and it pools at

my feet.

I'm left standing in a white lace bra, matching panties, thigh-high stockings and high-heeled white pumps.

Stefan looks me over, makes a sound from somewhere deep inside his chest. He steps backward. It's just one step, but it's enough for me to breathe again. I didn't realize I was holding my breath.

His gaze moves to the bra, to the delicate cups with the little red poppies on them. I remain still but my heart beats a marathon when he slides his knuckles over one lace-clad breast. My nipple hardens instantly.

He pushes against me and I feel him, feel his cock at my belly and the sound I make, it's not like his. It's not deep or threatening. It's more of a whimper.

His expression doesn't change as he slips his hand down over my belly and into my panties and when he cups my sex, my hands fly to his chest.

"Stefan!"

He watches me, and although I'm trying to push him off, I can't budge him. His fingers begin their work and his eyes bore into mine and fuck, it feels good. What he's doing feels good.

"I don't...I think...stop." That last word is so weak, I almost don't hear it myself.

And if he hears it, he doesn't stop.

Instead, he dips his head down and takes my nipple into his mouth, swallowing half my breast and I moan when he sucks, the lace rough, his mouth wet and soft and his fingers, God, his fingers.

A whimper catches in my throat and when he pulls his mouth away, I shudder at the loss, at the sudden cold. He straightens, leaning in closer, the scruff of his jaw rough against my cheek as he inhales deeply. He brings his mouth

to my ear and his fingers are doing something to me and I
don't want him to stop.

"You're wet," he whispers.

When he takes my clit between two fingers and
squeezes, I suck in a breath and my eyes close and I'm not
pushing him away anymore. I'm clinging to him.

"You're wet and I smell you," he says, voice low and deep
and I think his words become my undoing because he
knows. He knows I want this. Despite everything, I want
this. Want him.

He leans his face to mine and his lips brush my neck and
his fingers, fuck, his fingers. I'm going to come.

"Stefan," it's a gasp and my knees are wobbling. They're
going to give out.

He must know because all of a sudden, he lifts me in his
arms and he's laying me on his bed and he's dragging my
panties off.

My legs hang off the edge and he kneels on the floor
between them, pulling me to him, bending my knees back
to look at me for one long moment before closing his mouth
over my sex and devouring me whole. He's sucking and
licking and one hand moves upward, and when he takes my
nipple and squeezes it, I cry out because I'm coming. I'm
coming and I'm loud and desperate and the only word I
seem to remember at all is his name. His damned name.
Because I'm chanting it, breathless and out of my head and
out of this world, I am chanting his name as I come on his
tongue.

When it's finished, when I can think, I open my eyes
again, he straightens to his full height and wipes the back of
his hand across his mouth.

I feel my face burn and draw my legs in.

He looks me over, and I'm grateful he doesn't say

anything. Just looks. Because in his eyes, I see what he thinks. He's conquered me.

And he has, hasn't he?

He walks away and I sit up, watching him. From the bottle on the table across the room, he pours himself a tumbler of whiskey. He turns to me, drinks, watching me.

"Come here," he says.

I have a choice to make. I can let him own this night, or I can take it from him.

"Gabriela. I said come here."

And so, I make my choice.

I get to my feet. I'm naked but for my bra and stockings but I hold my head high as I walk to him and, without a word, I take his glass and I swallow the contents.

He's obviously surprised. One corner of his mouth curves upward and I set the glass down and wipe the back of my hand across my lips.

"Are you going to play games with me all night?" I ask, steeling myself, my voice strong. "Or are you going to fuck me?"

He grins, studying me. He unbuttons the top buttons of his shirt, pulls it out of his pants and undoes the cuffs before pulling it over his head.

I let my gaze wash over him the way his does me. No, worse.

I look him over like he's a piece of meat.

And I like the feeling.

I lay my fingernails on his hard chest and drag them down, meeting his gaze while I undo his belt, the button of his pants. I pull his zipper down a little, just enough to slide my hand inside and I keep my eyes locked on his as I cup his hard cock and squeeze.

I smile when Stefan sucks in a breath.

"I love that you call my name when you come," he says. He's trying to take it back, take back the night.

But I won't let him. "I like coming."

His grin widens. "Dirty girl." He takes my face in his hands, holds me as he brings his mouth to my ear and licks the shell of it. "I like dirty girls," he whispers, then takes the lobe between his teeth and when he draws it out, I feel it in my core and hear myself gasp and I want him. "I like doing dirty things to dirty girls."

I bring my mouth to his and kiss him. Almost. It's more a snapping of my teeth to taste the metallic taste of blood.

He moans, licking his own blood off his lip, and watches me as he slides his arms downward. He circles my wrists and it's like we're dancing a well-coordinated tango as he walks me backward to his bed. When the backs of my knees hit, I let myself drop down.

Stefan looms over me and I watch him strip off the rest of his clothes and fuck, he's beautiful, all hard muscle and power, his cock thick and ready and I'm not sure how I'm going to take that inside me.

When he's naked, when he's given me a good look, he sets his knees on the bed, lays his weight on top of me. He's heavy but it feels good.

"Why do you hate me?" I ask when he drags my arms over my head and holds them there with one of his.

"I don't hate you," he says, sliding his other arm down to open my legs. He pushes one thigh up. "I want to make you come again. I want to hear you call my name like that again."

I feel him then, at my entrance and that's when I falter. That's when I hesitate. I tug my arms, but he tightens his grip. Grins.

"You don't own this night, Gabriela. It's mine."

"Fuck you."

His grin is hungry and predatory. "I will fuck you. Just make sure you say my name again," he starts as he pushes the head of his cock inside me. "Scream it when you come on my dick."

He releases my wrists and I look between us, at it, at him and I try to push up, push away, but he's too big and too strong and he cups the back of my head and brings my face to his and kisses me, our eyes open, his hand fisting my hair.

"Stefan," I say it. I say his name as he pushes into me, stretching me.

It hurts. And it's going to get worse. I know it is. He's too big and he's not being gentle.

"Stefan," my voice sounds panicked.

He leans closer to me and my hand curls around the back of his head, fingers weaving into hair, pulling it hard.

"I want this. Wanted it for a long time," he says, lips on my lips, kissing. Biting. "I've wanted you for a long time."

He lets go of my hair and I grit my teeth as he closes his hands around mine. I curl my fingers around his, and my nails are digging into his skin, breaking it, drawing blood like he'll draw blood from me.

"It hurts," I manage.

"Look at me. Keep looking at me. Hurt me back," he says, forcing me to look at him, at his dark eyes, black ringed in gold and green. "Hurt me back."

I can't. I'm trying. But he's too big and I squeeze my eyes shut. "Stefan!"

"Look at me." He holds tight to me so I can't move. "Open your eyes and look at me, Gabi."

Gabi.

That name.

I open my eyes and lock them on his. I brace myself and

when he thrusts, I cry out and my cry is simultaneous to a tearing of skin, to that pouring of blood, that bleeding, more than I thought. A warm gush of it.

"Fuck." He draws back, does it again.

"Stefan!"

He's fucking me. He's fucking me hard and it hurts, and I don't want him to stop. I don't want him to let me go.

He kisses me again, sets his hands on either side of my head and lifts himself up a little to loom over me.

I grip his shoulders and he's so deep inside that I swear I feel him in my belly.

I can't drag my gaze from his and I don't think he can drag his from mine.

"Come for me," he says, sliding one hand down. When his fingers brush against my clit, I arch my back, wanting him, wanting his touch. Wanting to come.

Pain morphs and merges with pleasure and one intensifies the other, making it more. And when he moves inside me again and all I feel is him and the warmth of blood and his eyes on me, I come. I come again and I let out a long moan and it's his name on my tongue, my breath is his name.

He fucks me hard then, thrusting deep, taking and claiming in a way he hasn't yet. And when he stills, I feel his cock thickening, body tensing. He throbs inside me and I watch him come and I hear the sound he makes, and I feel him inside me. Feel him empty as he fills me up.

It's a few minutes later that he moves, blinks. His eyes aren't black anymore and the way he looks at me, it's the other Stefan. The one who carried me out of that well and what has he done to me? What's happened to me? What he said the other night, is he right? Am I falling in love with him? Have I already?

He watches me and I want to know what he sees because I don't know who I am anymore.

"Gabriela."

He slowly pulls out of me, and I feel every inch. I'm raw inside.

I follow his gaze down, feel semen slide out of me, see smeared blood on him. See it on my thighs, on the sheets.

He looks down too, shifts his weight to his knees. I pull back, can't seem to drag my eyes from all the blood, much more than I realized. The sheets are stained a deep red.

Stefan meets my gaze.

"Are you okay?" he asks, his voice hoarse.

I move to sit up, bite through the pain.

"Gabriela?"

I look at his shoulders, at the blood there. Small crescent shapes. My fingernails. I meet his eyes again. "I'm cold."

He gathers the blanket and puts it around my shoulders, then gets up, walks into the bathroom. A few minutes later, he's back and he sits own beside me. The blood is gone from him and in his hand is a damp towel.

I go to take it from him, but he shakes his head and he's cleaning me and he's gentle and tender and I just watch his dark head as he softly wipes the blood and cum from between my legs.

"I should have been more careful with you. Your first time..." he trails off, setting the towel aside.

I study him, see the weighted look in his eyes. And what I say, I don't say it to make him feel better. I say it because it's true.

"I don't know that it could have gone any other way. This is us, Stefan. This is you and this is me. It's always going to be this way with us."

19

STEFAN

I can't stop thinking about last night. About what she said. She's right. This is us. I will always take. And she will always be made to give.

"Exit's coming up," Rafa says beside me.

I nod, slowing the Bugatti down as I exit the highway and turn onto the smaller streets into Syracuse. I used to come here a lot growing up and know the streets pretty well. Avoiding the busiest part of the city, I make my way to the Greco house. It's in one of the poorer neighborhoods, which doesn't surprise me.

"Remind me again why do you want to do this?" Rafa asks me casually as we park outside the small, shabby house.

"Just want to hear for myself," I answer.

I found the man Gabriela recognized. I found his family. I expected them to be from Taormina, but it bodes well for my uncle that they're not.

"I already talked to them. There's nothing to hear, Stefan. His grandmother's an old woman who's now stuck raising two kids both under six. They don't know anything about Danny Greco. All they know is he's been gone for a while, which apparently isn't unusual for him."

Danny Greco is the name of the man who sideswiped Rafa's car. Who was one of the men at the house in Pentedattilo.

"Sounds like a class act." I get out of the car and look at the house. The plot is mostly sand, no grass, and the two trees are half-dead with thirst. Laundry blows in the hot wind on a line in the backyard which butts up to a crumbling concrete wall that divides it from the train running behind it.

All of the windows are open—I would be surprised if they had air-conditioning—and patterned curtains keep the sun and insects out.

This is poor Sicily. Where I live, how I grew up, I'm in the minority.

"Stef come on. We don't even have soldiers."

I look back at him. "Are you afraid of an old woman and two kids under six?"

He purses his lips and I get the feeling he wants to say something but decides to keep his mouth shut, which is a good thing.

I make my way up the street to the front door of the house and ring the doorbell. Here, too, a worn curtain with the same floral pattern billows. It's tucked into the locked metal gate that serves as a door.

It's two more rings before I hear little feet running toward us, kids speaking in rapid Italian, the one telling the other they're not supposed to open the door.

A moment later, two heads peer out from around the curtain. A boy and a girl.

"Is that your car?" the little boy asks. He appears to be the younger of the two.

Rafa chuckles.

I crouch down. "Yes, that's my car," I answer.

The boy whistles appreciatively. "A Bugatti. I prefer red. A real sports car."

"Do you?" Mine's black. I smile, straighten. "Is your grandmother home?"

The girl looks to her brother, then at me. She tries to shove him behind her and shakes her head in response to my question.

"She's at the market," the boy says, peering around her.

"Maybe we can wait for her out back."

"One minute," the girl says, then drops the curtain.

I stifle a laugh as they argue behind the curtain if it's wise or not to let us in. A few minutes later, the boy's head pops out from behind the curtain. "I'll open the garden gate."

"Good idea," I tell him, nodding.

"I think it was the Bugatti that got you points," Rafa says as he lights up a cigarette.

"When did you start smoking again?" I ask. He's quit several times, but the habit always manages to creep back up. I hate it, hate the smell of it.

He shakes his head like it's nothing and we walk around to where the boy opens the rickety fence and invites us into the backyard.

Two trains pass loudly by as we wait for the grandmother to return and the boy peppers me with questions about the car while the girl watches us with suspicion. Smart kid. It's when the third train is roaring past that the old woman returns pulling a trolley of food behind her. The moment she sees us, she stops dead, her face losing what little color it had.

I notice her glance settling a moment longer on Rafa than me and I step backward so I can see my cousin.

He busies himself with lighting another cigarette and the little girl yells at him to pick up his matches and the cigarette butt he already discarded.

I go to the woman, smile, introduce myself. She doesn't do me the same honor, but I let it go.

I take the trolley from her and drag it toward the house, noticing the broken wheel.

She takes it from me when we get inside.

I look around the small room. It never fails to shock me how poor poor can be. But then I see a photograph on the wall. I turn to her.

She shifts her gaze to Rafa who's hulking in the door.

"He's not here," she says before I even ask the question. She knows exactly why we're here.

"Who's not here?" I ask.

"Danny."

"This is Danny?" I ask, pointing to the photo.

She nods, looks me over in my suit. I know she wants to tell me to get the hell out, but she's smarter than that.

"Where is he?"

"Work." She puts a hand to her forehead and I see the worry in her eyes. "He didn't come back this time."

The kids come rushing in screaming about an ice-cream truck coming down the street and can they have a few dollars to buy one.

The grandmother starts to rush them back outside, away from us.

"Rafa, go buy the kids an ice cream."

"Are you fucking serious?"

"Watch your mouth." I gesture to the kids.

"No," the old woman says. "They don't go anywhere with either of you."

I stop her when she tries to grab the kids.

"They'll get ice cream. That's all."

She just glares at me and I gesture to Rafa to go ahead. He shakes his head but goes. The kids follow him, all smiles and excitement as they discuss which they'll choose.

I watch the old woman's eyes follow them.

"Do you know him?" I ask, gesturing to where Rafa just stood. I release her only when I'm sure she's not going to run after them.

She turns to me. Doesn't answer.

"Did Danny know him?" Better question, maybe.

"He dropped Danny off here a few times. I saw him in the car."

"When?"

"I don't remember. The children—"

"They're safe. You have my word."

She sighs, nods.

"Who was Danny working for?"

"I don't know. But that man," she shakes her head, makes the sign of the cross, then looks at me, makes it again. "Go. Please. We don't know anything. I haven't said anything. No police. The children, they're just children."

"I'm not here to hurt you or them," I say, processing what I've just learned.

"My son," she starts, shaking her head and pulling a chair out from the table. She sits down and I think about the amount of pressure she must be under. "I told him it was no good. Told him to get a decent job."

I don't care about her son. He hurt Gabriela. Put her in that well. But the children.

"How do you feed them?" I ask, looking around the kitchen.

She gives me a weary glance. "We manage."

I take out my wallet, pull out some bills and set them on the table.

She looks at the stack, then up at me and shakes her head. "Mafioso. I don't want your money."

"But you need it, so you'll take it."

We both hear the kids and I see the effort it takes her to school her features, to take the money and tuck it into the pocket of her dress and stand as the kids run in with their giant popsicles and huge smiles and hand her an unopened one.

"It's your favorite," the boy tells the old woman.

"Let's go," I tell Rafa, not missing how the woman looks at him. "You were right. Waste of time. She doesn't know a damn thing."

I don't even look back as I say it.

"Those kids need a fucking bath," Rafa says.

I get into the Bugatti and look over at my cousin.

He turns to me. "Let's get a drink. I'll call Clara."

"Don't call. We'll surprise her," I say, glancing in the rear-view mirror at the woman's face in the window as I pull away.

20

GABRIELA

How can two people living in the same house manage to avoid each other for days?

I should be grateful. Stefan hasn't been to see me since that night. Afterwards, after we lay in silence for an eternity, he got up and walked out of the room. His room. I slept alone and I don't know where he went but I haven't seen him since.

I'm watching the lovebirds from my place on the bed when there's a knock on the door early in the evening of the sixth night. I barely have a chance to sit up before Stefan opens the door. He stands there and looks at me, and I wonder if the crease between his eyebrows has become permanent.

I wonder if this is what he wanted out of this whole insane arrangement. Wonder if it's what he expected.

He may not hate me, but I wonder if he hates himself because the other night, he did what I predicted he would. He took.

But is what I did fighting?

Growing up in my father's world, you learn. Slowly or

quickly, you learn. You learn to take your lot and you plot your escape.

I think what's hardest is that I've stopped plotting. I'm not the fighter I was or thought I was.

In my father's house, I was alone.

In Stefan's house, I am alone.

I will always be alone. I think this is what hurts the most with him, because as much as I hate to admit it, it does hurt. I thought—I stupidly thought—he was different. I thought maybe together we wouldn't be alone.

Fuck. If I cry one more tear, I'm going to rip out my own tear ducts.

"What do you want?" I ask, getting off the bed to stand, using that moment to force those tears back.

He looks me over as he walks inside. I'm wearing a pair of white linen pants and a white sleeveless blouse. I'm barefoot.

I fold my arms across my chest as I wait for his reply.

"They're noisy," he says, walking to the bird cage.

"Let me take them away from here, then."

Three things surprise me then. The first is that he puts a finger inside the cage. The second is that the female bird goes to him. The third, and most strange, is that when she does, he gently caresses her.

"Did you name them?"

"She's Marguerite," I say, walking toward the table. "He's Mephistopheles."

Stefan pulls his hand out and looks at me with surprise. "Not Faust?"

"No. Faust loved Marguerite, even if that love was misguided. Mephistopheles represents the devil." He's clever enough to get my point. I walk away, out onto the balcony. "And the birds are not in love. She hates him."

"Dramatic," he says, joining me outside.

"I have time on my hands to think up the drama. What do you want?"

"The petition was granted. I'm your brother's legal guardian."

"Already?"

He nods.

I wonder how much money exchanged hands for that to happen.

"Congratulations," I say. "One more notch on your side of the who-can-be-a-bigger-asshole column. Does this mean you're in the lead?"

I see him bite back what he wants to say. His expression doesn't change, and I get the feeling he may be counting to ten. "Get packed, Gabriela. We're leaving for New York in a few hours."

"New York?" I say stupidly. I'm so surprised that it takes me a moment to process it. After that moment, though, surprise morphs into suspicion. "Why?"

"Don't you want to see Gabe? Celebrate his half-birthday?"

"How do you know about that?"

"Millie overheard you. Why didn't you tell me?"

"Why didn't I tell you about his half-birthday? Why would I? Why would I tell you anything that matters?"

"Gabriela," he starts. He reaches out to me but I draw back. He drops his arm and walks to the railing.

I watch him stand there, looking out over the sea, and I think how different this could have been. How different I wish it were.

When he turns to me, his features are schooled. "I thought you might want to bring him here. Would you like that?"

What? He's asking if I want to bring my brother here?

"Gabe? Bring him here as in Sicily? To live with us?"

He nods.

I'm shocked.

"Why? What game are you playing?"

"I'm not playing any game."

"How does it benefit you?"

"It doesn't."

"Then why? Why would you do that?"

"Because you're sad and your brother makes you happy."

Fuck.

Tears burn my eyes and I turn my face away. "Why do you do this?" I ask, unable to keep the quaver from my voice.

He comes to me, stands behind me and puts his hands on the railing on either side of me. He's so close, I can smell his cologne, the same one he always wears. I can feel the heat of his body. And some part of me, some stupid, masochistic part of me, it wants to lean into him. Wants to lay my head on his shoulder and let him hold me.

"It would be easier if you were just one way," I say. "I don't have the strength to keep up with you." My breath trembles when I draw it in.

He wraps his arms around me and when he does, I can't help but do what I wanted to do. I lean back into him. Because what I said, it's worse than that.

I have no more strength *period*. I'm done fighting.

"I want to be the man you want, Gabriela. I want to be the man who carried you out of that well."

I turn in his arms, look up at him.

He puts his hands on my face, and he's so big, so much bigger than me. My protector and my predator in one. He pushes my hair back, smearing tears across my cheeks. He looks down at me and what I see in his eyes, it makes me ache.

"Hope is a stupid thing," I say.

He's caught off guard and it takes him a moment. "No, it's not a stupid thing. It's a good thing. And sometimes, the only thing. I don't want you sad anymore, Gabriela. This isn't your father's house. This isn't anything but what you let it be."

"You don't know how much I want to believe you."

"Then believe me."

He kisses me then and it takes me a minute. It takes me that minute to register his lips on mine. His mouth on mine. His breath, his warm mouth, his strong arms. It's not erotic or sexual. It's different. Soft. A consummation of trust, so much more important than the consummation of our marriage.

It takes me a full minute to accept that kiss because my mind wanders to where it had gone the other night. To that question. And I know the answer.

He warned me not to fall in love with him but it's too late. I think it was too late a long time ago.

"Stefan," I start, drawing back. I have to stop this. Because after everything this is the thing that will break me.

He closes his mouth over mine again and doesn't release me from his kiss as he walks me backward to my bed. When the backs of my knees hit it, I drop down to a seat and he crouches, kissing me with a hunger that matches my own. A need that matches my own.

He's not careful undressing me. Something tears as he strips my pants and panties off and he's between my legs, one hand on the top of my head, the other undoing his jeans, his eyes fierce and dark and their expression the same as when he looked at me out there on that balcony.

And when he pushes into me, I'm ready for him. I cling to him and hear his grunt, feel him, his big body on top of mine, his thick cock inside me, stretching me, hurting me, making me his as I cleave to him and wrap my legs around him and our kiss, it's need. Pure need. A possession. Like we can't get enough. Can't get close enough.

When I come, it's different than any other time. With him. By myself. It's different and whole and I don't close my eyes or turn away. I watch him and let him watch me and something is different between us. Maybe it's us who are different. I just know I can't be without him.

And I know if he betrays me again, it will destroy me.

21

STEFAN

Tucked beneath a blanket, Gabriela is asleep in the seat beside mine as we fly through the night sky to the states. She has her head turned toward me and her hands are tucked beneath her cheek.

She looks so young when she sleeps. So innocent and vulnerable.

The flight attendant comes with my drink and I turn to take it, thanking her with a nod. I sit in the dimly lit cabin and sip as I think.

There's more than one reason we're going to New York. Yes, I want to get her brother for her. I don't want anything from Gabe Marchese. Yes, he's a pawn. And yes, I wanted guardianship out of selfish reasons. But if the end result makes her happy while meeting my goals, then so be it and I am happier for it.

I meant what I said. I want to be the man who carried her out of the well.

It's just complicated.

Those of us who crawl out of the darkness, we're never fully able to stand in the light for long.

The bird cage was made by a goldsmith in New York City. The cost wouldn't be something my uncle could afford to pay himself. But I believe he had a patron.

If I'm right, then it confirms that my uncle is my enemy.

My mind drifts to my meeting with Danny Greco's mother. To how she looked at Rafa. To how she remembered him.

I glance over at my cousin.

He must feel my eyes on him because he turns his head. There's a moment of nothing. Then he nods before looking away.

———

THE DRIVER TAKES US TO THE HOTEL WHEN WE ARRIVE. CLEAR Meadows is an hour drive from here and Gabriela's excitement is palpable. If it were up to her, we'd go straight there, but I want to go with her, and I first need to shower, change and meet with the goldsmith.

I'm having Rafa take her to a shop to buy Gabe a half-birthday present and two soldiers have been instructed to follow Rafa and Gabriela. I won't take any chances with her, but I wouldn't leave him in Sicily either.

If it were anyone else, I would already have taken care of it. I wouldn't ask any more questions. But Rafa, he's been a brother to me. We grew up together. He stood by my side during my family's fall. And I don't like questioning his loyalty.

"I'm ready," Gabriela says when I walk out of the bathroom with a towel wrapped around my hips, still dripping from my shower.

She's beaming.

I haven't seen her this happy in, well, I've never seen her this happy.

I go to her, take her arms and tug her to me. "The shops haven't even opened yet," I tell her, looking her over. She's wearing a light pink halter dress that comes to just above her knees and a pair of flat sandals. "You look good, Gabriela."

Her gaze slides down to my bare chest, to the tattoo over my heart. Her fingertips brush over the skin there.

"Did it hurt?"

I shrug.

She slides her fingers lower to the thick scar tissue. "How about this one?"

"That one did. But I needed it."

She looks up at me. "What do you mean?"

"It taught me a valuable lesson." I kiss her.

"What lesson?"

I smile, kiss her again, turn her around and lift her hair to untie the bow that's keeping the dress up.

"Stefan," she starts, glancing over her shoulder at me. "We don't have time."

"We have time," I say, turning her to face me and kissing her. "And I want to take my time."

She's not wearing a bra and I cup one breast while walking her backward to the bed. I don't put her on it though. Instead, when her knees hit it, I put one hand to her shoulder and push her to kneel.

She looks up at me with those pretty, huge eyes. Innocent eyes.

I think how I'm going to dirty her.

Leaning down, I kiss her mouth, dropping my towel as I do. I weave my fingers into her hair and tug her head backward.

"I owe you a lesson," I whisper. "I promised to teach you how to suck my cock."

I draw back, straighten and look down at her, at those greedy eyes she's unable to keep from my dick, at her hungry little tongue that darts out to lick her lips.

"Open, baby," I say. "And kiss my cock." She obeys, first licking precum off before kissing the head then taking me into her mouth.

That's not going to be enough for me today though.

I grin, lean into her so the bed supports the back of her head. I guide myself deeper.

"I'm going to need a little more, sweetheart," I say, sliding in and out slowly, feeling the warm, soft, wet mouth, seeing the panic in her eyes as I tilt her head back to go deeper.

Her hands come to my thighs and tears form at the corners of her eyes.

I hold there. Watch her like this.

"Do you trust me?" I ask, drawing back just a little, just enough for her to catch a breath before pushing in again, deeper this time, touching the back of her throat. "Do you?" I pull out, force her head back. "Do you trust me, Gabriela?"

She considers for a long minute and fuck my timing. I want to be back inside her. Back inside her warm, hot little mouth.

Finally, she nods.

I smile, slide my cock in again, pump in and out twice more before pulling out and leaning down to kiss her.

"That's good," I whisper. "Because you're going to need to trust me when I fuck your face." I straighten, grip a handful of hair and tug her head backward as I set one foot on the edge of the bed and push into her.

She says something, I think it's my name, but it sounds gurgled.

"Fuck, you are so pretty with my cock stuffed inside your mouth. Put your fingers on your pussy and rub your clit," I tell her.

I wait, watching as she does as she's told and when I hear the wet sounds of her pussy, I fuck her face hard, giving her everything, watching her take it, take me. Watching her swallow down my seed as she comes on her sticky little fingers.

22

GABRIELA

I'm disappointed that it's Rafa who takes me out to buy Gabe a gift while Stefan goes to an appointment. Rafa seems as pleased as I am to have to babysit me.

"I can go on my own," I say. I know the city. I know what I want to buy my brother and from where to buy it.

"No, you can't," he says as the driver drops us off in front of the boutique toy store. "You're Stefan's wife now. You need protection."

"You seem about as happy to babysit me as I am to be babysat."

He rolls his eyes.

"Rafa, did I do something to you that made you dislike me?"

I'm not sure he's surprised by the question.

"He likes you, that's all."

Is he jealous? He must see the confusion and surprise on my face because he shakes his head.

"I mean it gives his enemies a target. A way to hurt him."

I study him and what I see in his eyes, it's a war. Rafa is

fighting some battle and I think Stefan and I and what we just discussed is a part of that battle.

I reach out and touch his hand. "You're a good friend to him."

He doesn't reply, doesn't even look at me.

"I'll be in in a minute," he finally says. "Just going to have a smoke."

He's dismissing me.

"Is everything okay?" I ask.

He opens the door, steps out. "Fine." He gestures to the door of the old shop and I go to it, push it open, hearing the bell over the door. The instant that door closes behind me, I'm transported to another world.

This is where my mom bought our gifts when we were growing up and after her death, for reasons I don't wholly understand, my father kept up the tradition. He probably had someone do the shopping for him, but still, he did it. And even though the gifts were bitter sweet after mom died, they were still special.

"Gabriela Marchese?" comes a familiar voice. "Is that you?"

I look up at the register set on a raised, dark wooden platform, and through the high-quality puppets and dolls and old-fashioned register, I see Mr. Poe.

I smile, go to him.

"Mr. Poe, you're still working the register?" I ask as the tiny man walks around the counter, down the steps and toward me. He's gotten older, the big bush of curly black hair now salt-and-pepper. And he's slightly hunched, which makes him appear even shorter than his five feet.

"Well, well," he says, hands on his hips, looking me over from head to toe. "Gabriela, I don't believe it. All grown up."

He leans in to hug me and I hug him back. "I knew you'd be a beauty, but my goodness!"

When we separate, he holds onto my hands and spies the rings on my wedding finger.

"Some lucky man already snatched you up? I'm not surprised," he says. He touches the diamond. "He values you."

I'm not sure about that last part. Maybe?

"You're blushing, my dear. Tell me how you've been."

We spend the next fifteen minutes talking. Well, I do most of the talking while he listens. When he hands me a piece of candy from the old-fashioned jar he still keeps on the counter, it takes me back in time.

"What can I do for you?" he asks as I look at that candy, unwilling to eat it, not sure I'll be able to without breaking down. Being in here reminds me of my mom. Of when things were good.

"I'm here for Gabe's half-birthday gift," I say.

I see the flash of something like regret that crosses his features. "How is your brother? I remember how rambunctious he was when your mother would bring him in here to pick out a new toy."

"He's doing all right. I'm going to move him to Sicily so we'll be closer together."

"Are you all the way in Sicily now? Such a long way from your father."

I just smile.

"Well, come on now. I seem to recall a particular toy train your brother loved and there's a new model. You think he'll like it?" he asks, taking me to the section of trains.

I pick up the box he points to. "I think he'll love it. And maybe something for painting? It's his new hobby, it seems."

"Well, painting is good for the soul. I have just the thing."

Stefan gave me his credit card to pay for the things and it's weird doing so. Weird to use his money. Will I always be dependent on him?

Mr. Poe wraps the packages carefully, choosing special paper and huge bows for the boxes. As I gather the packages in my arms, I think how happy Gabe will be. How surprised. I never told him I was coming. And I can't wait to get there.

"One more thing," Mr. Poe says as I'm readying to say goodbye. He goes behind the counter and rummages through a cabinet beneath the register. I hear him mutter and a moment later, his head pops up. "Here we are."

He walks back around the counter toward me and holds out his hand. I look down at the small ring on his finger.

"What's this?" I ask, touching the dragon shape.

"A mood ring. I remember you loved these when you were little."

I take it from him, smiling. "I haven't seen one of these in ages."

"You used to tell me you'd know when someone was lying when you wore one."

I slide it on my little finger, touch the smooth green stone. I know this isn't an ordinary mood ring. The design is too intricate for that.

"Thank you, Mr. Poe. I love it."

"You're welcome, Gabriela." He hugs me back. He's barely released me when Rafa surprises us both by walking out of a door that leads to the stock room. The look on his face tells me something is wrong.

"Rafa? What is it?"

Mr. Poe stares at him open-mouthed.

"We have to go," he says and when he moves, I see the

glint of shiny metal in a shoulder holster and the smudge of red on his knuckle.

"What's happened?" I ask as he takes my arm.

"There were men following. And we're outnumbered. We need to go. Now."

"But—"

"Now!"

I almost drop the boxes as he pulls me along out through the stock room and into an alley where our SUV awaits minus the driver. He opens the passenger door, his expression as he turns his gaze to the mouth of the alley making me panic.

"What's happening?" I ask.

Once I'm in, he slams the door shut and runs to the driver's side, gets in, and a moment later, we're peeling out of the alley, cars honking their horns wildly as we merge with traffic. I let out a scream, catching myself on the dashboard and the door, all of this reminiscent of the last time I was in a car with Rafa.

"Put your seatbelt on," he snaps, eyes on the rear-view mirror as he takes an illegal left.

I look back, but I can't tell who's who. All I see is a road full of cars, trucks and taxis.

"Who is it?" I ask, putting on my belt.

"I don't know," he says, just glancing at me as the car hits a pothole. "I think I lost them."

"Did you call Stefan?"

He glances at me, nods. "It's okay, Gabriela. We lost them. You can relax now."

I lean my head against the headrest. "Is it always going to be like this?"

"He has many enemies."

I process that as we leave the city.

"Where are we going now?" I ask. I know this area pretty well. I didn't realize he did.

"I'll take you to your brother."

"That's the other way. We have to go north on—"

"I know where we have to go. I don't want to take a chance anyone is following us."

Stefan's words echo along with the warning bells that ring wildly in my head.

There's nothing nice about Rafa.

I dig into my bag, pull out my cell phone.

"What are you doing?" he asks.

"I want to call Stefan."

"It's not necessary. He's in a meeting."

I scroll through the few numbers to find Stefan's. I'm about to hit the call button when Rafa's hand closes over mine, the pressure just a little harder than it needs to be.

"I told you that's not necessary," he says.

"You're hurting me."

He loosens his hold, shifts his gaze back to the dense traffic as he slides the phone out of my hands and puts it in the center console.

"Where are you taking me, Rafa?" I ask when we take a turn in the direction of the Verrazano Bridge.

"I told you. I'll take you to see your brother. After."

"After what?"

We get to a traffic light and when it turns yellow, the car in front of us stops.

Rafa mutters a curse and as soon as we're slow enough, I reach to undo my seatbelt and open the door at once, but he's too fast and when his hand closes over my arm, his grip is bruising, punishing.

"I don't want to hurt you, Gabriela," he says.

"Let me go!"

Traffic begins to move, and he doesn't let me go as he moves with them.

"Where are you taking me?" I struggle against him but he's too strong.

"Your father."

"Why? Let me go!"

Cars honk their horns as he swerves through two lanes to come to an abrupt stop on the shoulder. He squeezes his hand and gives me a shake. "I'll take you to your brother after. I won't let anyone hurt you."

"You're hurting me now. I don't want to see my father. I want Stefan!"

As soon a I say Stefan's name, his gaze turns icy. "Stefan isn't the man you think he is. You need to hear what your father has to tell. Are you going to give me trouble? I don't want to have to knock you out."

"Knock me out?"

"I said I don't want to—"

"But you will."

He gives an exasperated sigh, shifts his grip to my jaw, his fingers digging into my skin and with one quick jerk, the back of my head smashes against the window and all I see before I pass out is Rafa's face, the emotions warring in his eyes, the regret and the rage. All I see is Stefan's trusted cousin, his right-hand man as my vision fades.

23

GABRIELA

"Christ. I didn't tell you to beat her."

"I didn't beat her. She's fine. She's already coming to."

"Gabriela?" My father's voice sounds unusual. Tender, almost.

I blink my eyes open, but when I move, the back of my head throbs. I reach a hand to the spot, feel the bump, remember how I got it the instant Rafa comes into view looming behind my father.

I startle, my eyelids flying open.

"It's all right. He won't touch you again," my father says as he stands, giving Rafa a hateful glance.

I look around, sit up. I'm in the living room of the Todt Hill house, half-lying half-sitting on a chaise. I sit up, lick my lips. I'm parched.

"Here," my father hands me a glass of water.

I take it, drink two sips and watch Rafa walk away, shaking his head. He leans against the far wall and watches me, his eyebrows furrowed together, the look in his eyes dark.

"Don't look at him," my father says, taking the water glass from me and setting it aside. "He won't lay a finger on you ever again. Fucking Sicilian brutes."

"Be careful, old man," Rafa warns.

My father doesn't even bother turning toward him, instead, he takes the seat across from mine.

"You're going to see Gabe."

"I was."

"Don't you think to come to visit your father when you're in town? Why, I wonder?"

I blink, shift my gaze. I know this answer.

"That's right. Because you helped your bastard husband steal my son out from under me."

"Gabe isn't a thing to steal. He's a human being."

"Hmm," he says, cocking his head to the side. "You of all people should know better than that by now, Gabriela." He glances at Rafa. "All things can be bought in our world. And all things that can be bought can also be stolen. *You stole my son out from under me.*"

"You locked *your son* away after making him what he is. Do you know that people think Gabe is dead? You don't even acknowledge him as your son anymore."

I see the twitch in his eye, the tell-tale sign that what I just said got to him.

He breathes in a deep breath and stands.

I would stand too, but I'm a little dizzy.

"Why am I here?" I ask.

"Because I miss you," he says.

"Liar."

He grins, a coldness seeping into his eyes. "You're here because you did something very stupid."

I stare up at him.

"Are you playing house out there in that Sicilian hole?

Are you spreading your legs for that bastard? For *our* enemy?"

I bolt to my feet and have to fight the dizziness. "I'm leaving!"

My father steps toward me and it takes all I have to remain standing. "You'll leave when I'm finished. Now sit down."

I don't.

He leans into me. "Sit. Down."

I want to say I do it because I'm dizzy but it's a lie. Only when I'm down does he step away.

"You're more and more like your mother every day, you know that?"

"Don't talk about mom."

"She was a traitor too," he says, ignoring me, looking like a giant as he looms over me and all I can think is I wish Stefan were here. I wish he were standing between us.

"And you taught her, didn't you?" I say, bitterness edging the words.

He gives an odd grin, exhales and walks to the liquor cabinet to pour himself a drink. He doesn't offer Rafa or me one, not that I'd take it.

"You killed her." It's strange how it sounds when it's said out loud like that. Just a fact. Just words.

My father's back is to me. I watch as he lifts the glass to drink.

"I saw," I say. I don't mean to whisper but that's how quietly the words come. "I saw it all."

I shudder and the sudden cold makes the tiny hairs on my arms stand on end.

He turns to face me, and, in my periphery, I can see Rafa and I wonder what he'd do if my father pounced on me now. Would he help me? Or would he stand back and watch?

"You were hiding? Spying?"

"You don't deny it?" I know this truth. I've known it for years. Why does it hurt when he doesn't tell me I'm crazy? Tell me I don't know what I'm talking about and that I remember wrong because he'd never hurt my mother.

"I loved her. I love her still. She never listened, though. Stubborn as a mule. Like you."

God. Why is this so hard to hear when I've known all along?

"I want to go now," I say to Rafa.

My father finishes his drink and pours another. "It was an accident."

Here it is. The denial. His too late denial.

"An accident? You held her under the water. I remember."

"She made me very angry, Gabriela."

"So it was her fault?"

"She was fucking a soldier. The man I paid to keep her safe." His voice is tight. I know that tone. It's the one that says the rage beneath is just barely leashed. It's the one that says to tread lightly. Or better yet, run for cover.

But I can't run right now. I don't even want to. Lies, lies and more lies. This is my life. Betrayal and hate and lies.

"I loved her," he says, coming toward me again. "I loved her so much." His eyes are momentarily distant, and I think he did love her. In his way. In his suffocating, smothering way. When his eyes come back into focus, they're intent on me. "And I love you even more, Gabriela. I'll do anything for you. Anything."

A shudder runs through me and I hear Rafa's muttered curse. He must see how fucked up this is. He must see he shouldn't have brought me here.

Rafa stands. The moment he does, I hear footsteps

behind me and turn to find John and another of my father's men step toward us. I didn't realize they were even there. Did they hear what I just said? Did they hear Gabriel Marchese just admit to having murdered his wife?

It doesn't matter. They'll still protect him. It's just like my father said and he is right, I do know that. Everything and everyone can be bought and sold and stolen and drowned in our world. Honor is what's missing. Conscience.

"I'm taking her," Rafa says.

"No, you're not. Not until she hears what I need to tell her."

"Be quick about it, then."

My father turns to Rafa. "Be careful, Rafa, is it?"

Rafa grits his teeth.

"You're a traitor too, Rafa. She knows it now. You'll want her to hear so she doesn't go running to tell her *husband* the truth—the whole truth—because I think he'll murder you with his bare hands if he finds out what you did to his precious wife."

Precious.

There's that word again from forever ago.

I'm not precious to anyone. Don't they know that yet? I know it.

Something twists inside me and my chest tightens.

"Gabe is waiting. Tell me," I tell my father.

He turns to me. "Do you know why Stefan wanted guardianship? All of a sudden? When he's never given a shit about your brother?"

"Because you wanted to cut me off from him. Stefan's not the monster you claim he is, so you wanted to take away the one person who matters and make it look like it was Stefan's doing."

One corner of his mouth lifts into a smirk.

"You killed Alex. Gabe is all I have left," I add.

"Alex?" he seems genuinely surprised. "You think that was me?" He chuckles, shakes his head at me and I realize something. He's telling the truth.

"If I wanted him dead, I would have done it the day I had his legs broken. Think, Gabriela. What would I have to gain from killing the boy and his aunt? What?"

Nothing.

"Tell me what you want to tell me and let me go," I say. I don't like this. Don't like where it's going.

He smiles, drinks a sip of his drink and sets his glass down.

"So you believe Stefan took my son for you? Because he *cares* about you? Because he wants you to be happy?"

I remember Stefan's words. *"I don't want you sad anymore, Gabriela."*

"Stop playing with me. Say it. Say it or I'm leaving."

"He did it because I cut you off. Because I named Gabe as sole beneficiary of the Marchese inheritance. He did it to steal that inheritance. And you helped him. You just signed on the dotted line, you stupid, stupid girl."

24

STEFAN

By the time I see Rafa's call come in an hour after my men lost them, I'm beside myself and pissed as fuck.

"Where the fuck is she?" I bark when the call connects.

"She's fine. We're fine."

I could give a damn about him.

"Where are you?"

"We're at Clear Meadows. She just walked into her brother's room. We were being followed, Stefan. I took her out the back of the toy store."

I grit my teeth because I can't tell him those men were my men. That I was having him followed because I didn't trust him with Gabriela.

"Why did it take you so long to call me?"

"I was busy trying to lose them. Traffic's insane in this city. I didn't realize it had been so long."

"Is she okay?"

"Yeah. Shaken, but she's fine."

"Let me talk to her."

"They just brought out the cake."

Fuck. I suck in a deep breath. "I'm on my way."

"You don't have to come. I'll bring her back—"

"I'll be there in forty minutes. Neither of you leaves." I disconnect the call. I don't want to talk to Rafa right now.

My meeting ended later than expected, but I learned more than I was ready for.

I knew Marchese was involved. I knew he wouldn't take any of this lying down. But my uncle's betrayal—does it mean he was behind Gabriela's kidnapping? And was Rafa either aware or involved in it?

I need to think. Process. Decide on how to move forward.

But first, Gabriela.

We pull up to Clear Meadows forty minutes later and Rafa greets me at the door. I study him, try to read him. He seems shifty. Not quite the Rafa I have an easy relationship with. But am I seeing what I want to see?

"Where is she?"

"I'll take you to her. I think they're getting ready to wrap up."

I follow Rafa through the front entrance through to a main room where balloons bounce along the ceilings and streamers decorate the green walls. Patients are gathered, most in pajamas, some in wheelchairs, many eating cake.

Gabriela stands beside her brother at the front of the room. He towers over her, and beside him, she looks so small. I wonder if that's how she and I look together.

There's almost no resemblance between them but their affection is visible, even from this distance and I'm glad I brought her here. I'm glad she has this.

She's holding her hand out and Gabe is looking at something. I wonder if it's her engagement ring but realize it's her right hand.

When I take a step toward them, she sees me. At first, it's

surprise I see on her face. She stares at me, eyes wide, face paling a little.

I expected a smile. Relief at the very least.

But maybe this is residue of what happened. Of what happened on my watch *again*.

Gabe follows her gaze and turns to me. I look at him, at this man with the mind of a boy. I see it, too. It's in his eyes, the damage. I wonder what it takes for a father to do this to his son. And I wonder if death isn't more merciful.

"Who is that man?" I hear him ask Gabriela.

She smiles, takes his hand and leads him toward me.

"Gabriela," I say. When I lean in to kiss her cheek, she leans away, gives a slight shake of her head.

"This is Stefan, the friend I was telling you about," she says.

The word 'friend' is hard to swallow.

"He gave you the shiny ring," Gabe says.

She nods. "Yes. That's him."

Gabe smiles at me. "It's a pretty ring."

"Thank you," I say. "It's not as pretty as Gabriela though."

"Nothing is as pretty as Gabi," he says. He studies me for a long moment and it's unnerving because there's a flicker of Marchese in his gaze. A moment of knowing. But then he extends his hand. "I'm Gabe."

"It's very nice to meet you, Gabe. Happy half-birthday."

His smile widens and he turns to Gabriela. "I want another slice of cake," he says.

"That sounds like a good plan." We watch him walk away.

"Are you all right?" I ask Gabriela. "Rafa told me what happened."

She turns to me, her gaze cautious. A little sad. "I don't

think it's a good idea to bring Gabe to Sicily," she starts, surprising me.

"I thought you'd want him close."

"I want to move him from here, but I don't want him near us."

Bullshit. "Be more specific, Gabriela. Say what you mean."

She studies me, searches my face, my eyes. "I don't want him near you."

Her words have the impact of a fist to the gut.

"This morning just shows how dangerous it can be," she adds.

"This morning shouldn't have happened."

"But it did happen. Just like my kidnapping happened. Just like my being put at the bottom of a well happened."

I cut my gaze to the right, find Rafa standing at the door watching us.

"We'll talk about it," I say.

"What's to talk about? I'm not safe. How could my brother ever hope to defend himself if your enemies came after him?"

"We'll talk later, Gabriela."

"No. We won't. I've decided."

"I said we'll talk. Go and enjoy some time with your brother."

"Gabriela," a woman comes over, cautiously glancing at me. "We should wrap this up. This surprise has been a lot on Gabe. I think he should rest."

"Okay. Let me just say goodbye."

The woman nods and Gabriela slips away, hugs her brother and whispers something in his ear. When she walks back toward me, she's carrying two paintings. Well, they're more of a child's drawings on canvas.

"Gabe made these. This one's for me and this one's for Alex. I promised I'd take it to him."

I just look at them because what can I say?

"He's asking why Alex hasn't FaceTimed him lately."

"What did you tell him?"

"I lied. Said Alex was probably busy."

"I'm sorry you had to do that."

I know from the way she's looking at me something's up. Not sure what, but something.

After waving goodbye to Gabe, I walk her outside where she stops me before we get into the car. I notice when she scratches the back of her head, she winces.

"What is it?" I reach to touch it.

She pulls away. "Nothing."

"It's not nothing. You're acting strange," I say, putting my fingers to the spot, feeling the bump there. "And this isn't nothing."

"I hit my head during the chase." She shifts her gaze away.

I cock my head to the side, trying to work it through. "How did you hit the *back* of your head?"

"I wasn't wearing my seatbelt and was turned around. I hit it against the passenger side window."

I study her, trying to figure out how that could physically happen. But why would she lie to me? She has no reason to.

"Everything okay?" I ask.

"No, it's not. Not at all. How can you think it can be? Where were you this morning? What meeting did you have? And is that the only reason you brought me? Because you were coming anyway? I thought we were coming for Gabe. I thought we'd see him together."

"We did see him together."

"It's not what I mean."

"We'll talk at the hotel."

"No, we'll talk now."

"I understand that you were scared. But you're safe now. I'm not going to let anything happen to you again."

"You've told me that before Stefan. You've said those exact words. You can't keep me safe. Don't you get it?" Her voice climbs up an octave. "Being around you is dangerous for me. It's dangerous for my brother."

I close my hand over hers, count to ten as I squeeze it.

"I said we will talk at the hotel, Gabriela. Am I not clear enough?"

"You're perfectly clear, Stefan."

She turns to the window, and we ride in silence to the hotel. Once we're in our suite, she walks directly into the bedroom and would slam the door shut if I didn't catch it.

"What the fuck is going on, Gabriela?"

She spins on her heel, stalks back toward me. "Why don't you tell me?"

"It's been a long fucking day."

She opens her mouth, but closes it again, and I feel like she's full of words, full of seething, burning anger.

"Talk to me," I tell her.

"Leave me alone. After everything that's happened, I don't feel much like talking to you. Just go."

I snort. "Are you dismissing me?"

"Yeah. I guess I am. Get out. I mean it."

I go to her, walk her backward to the wall, press my chest to hers to keep her pinned.

"I'm not going anywhere. Now tell me why you're acting like a spoiled little bitch."

"Fuck you!"

I slam my hands into the wall on either side of her head and she jumps.

"Fuck off?" I ask.

"Let me go. Get away from me." She shoves at my chest.

"Say it again," I order.

Her gaze burns.

"I dare you. Say it again."

"No."

"No?" I ask, reaching to undo my belt, my jeans. I watch her as her eyes flit downward, as her breathing comes in short gasps. "But I want to fuck you. I want you to say it so I can give you what you want."

"That's not—"

I grip her hips, lift her off the ground. With my chest against hers, I keep her there as I reach to push the crotch of her panties over.

"Let me go," she says, her tone weaker than it was a moment ago.

She digs her nails into my back, the shirt I'm wearing too thin to offer much protection.

I brush my fingers over her wet pussy. "I don't think you want me to let you go."

"I do."

I rub two fingers over her clit, and she closes her eyes, hands in my hair now, pulling at it.

"Liar," I tell her.

"You're the liar," she accuses as I thrust into her.

"Am I?" I ask, taking both legs and pushing them up toward the wall, opening her, pulling out to spear her again.

"Let me go," she gasps.

"You're mine. I'm not letting you go anywhere," I say, shifting one hand to grip the hair at the back of her head, seeing her wince when I force her head backward. "Tell me something, how do you get a bump at the back of your head when you're in a car chase? If you were turned around, you'd have hit the side of your face. Not the back of your head."

"Let me go." She pushes against me.

"I already told you. I'm not letting you go." I thrust, draw out. "I'm never letting you go."

I bring my mouth to hers and kiss her and she bites my lip hard, drawing blood.

I pull back, keeping her impaled while I wipe the blood with two fingers. I smear it across her lips then kiss her again, deep and hard, the way I'm fucking her.

Taking her hands, I intertwine my fingers with hers and draw them up over her head, pulling back a little to look at her, feeling her wrap her legs around me, feeling them tighten.

"You make me crazy you know that?" I say, tasting my blood on her when I kiss her again. "I should pull out of you. Not let you come. I should force you to your knees and come on your face and make you stay there like that, watch you on your knees with my come all over your face."

"I hate you," she says through gritted teeth, moving with me, taking her pleasure.

"You love me," I say, and there's a moment, a split second where we both stop. Where we're suspended in time. And I look at her sea-foam colored eyes and I think it's true.

"I'll never love you," she says, her voice strange as she wraps her arms around me, closing those eyes, burying her face in my shoulder and grinding against me. "Never."

"Liar."

I thrust deep inside her, carry her to the bed and lay her on her back and I fuck her so hard that when she comes, she's not whispering my name. She's screaming it.

25

GABRIELA

Before we leave the next morning, I find myself alone with Rafa in a corner of the lobby.

Stefan's on a call. He's in another part of the lobby, his back to us. I watch him as I talk to Rafa.

"Are you okay?" he asks.

I shift my gaze to his. "Am I okay? You fucking asshole. Am I fucking okay? No. I'm not okay. Not even a little okay."

"I meant what I said. I'll help you hide him, at least."

After leaving my father's house yesterday, Rafa made a proposition. I don't know if it was out of guilt or if he felt somehow sorry at how fucked up my relationship with my father is or what, but he told me he'd help me get Gabe out of Clear Meadows and put him somewhere safe. Somewhere neither Stefan nor my father would know about. I don't know if he thought that would make it okay or make me trust him or if he gives a fuck if I do, but I do know that if I manage to hide Gabe away, not my father or Stefan or Rafa can know where. Each one of these men is as dangerous as the other.

I realize he's still talking a moment later. "Help you if you need any—"

"Help me against Stefan? He trusts you and you betrayed him. For my father. He'll kill you if he finds out."

"He's not going to find out."

"Are you so sure?"

"You didn't tell him. And I don't think you will."

"Don't be so cocky. It doesn't suit you. Was anyone even following us? Or was that part of your trick?"

He doesn't answer and all I can think is what a fool I am. How easy to manipulate.

I school my features when Stefan glances our way. I don't bother smiling. I don't know what I'm going to do. All I know is they're all liars, Stefan, my father, Rafa. Each one has betrayed me. Some more than once.

"How much did my father pay you, anyway?"

"It's not like that."

"Then what's it like? Explain it to me. Explain why you'd betray the man who thinks of you as a brother."

He looks at me with a sick expression on his face and reaches into his pocket to grab his pack of cigarettes. "You don't know anything, Gabriela." He brushes past me, knocking my shoulder when he does.

"What was that about?" Stefan asks.

I turn and am surprised to find him so close. He was at the far end of the room not a moment ago.

"Nothing," I say, looking up at him. He's in a suit again, his usual dress code even for travel. I'm still processing what I learned yesterday. Still processing this, his latest betrayal.

When he looks down at me, I shift my gaze away.

He touches a finger underneath my chin and tilts my face up to his.

"What's the matter?" he asks. "What's happened since yesterday afternoon?"

My heart hurts at his words. At his tone. At the look in his eyes that I can't trust. That I so badly want to—*wanted to*—trust.

I jerk out of his reach. "Nothing. Can we go?" I say, simultaneously turning, taking a step back.

He grabs my arm, stopping me, making me look over my shoulder at him. "Something. Tell me."

I just stare back at him. With my father, I didn't suck at lying. At pretending. Although with him, we both knew how I felt about him.

With Stefan, it's different. I have to pretend. He can't know that I saw my father yesterday. He can't know that I know why he wanted guardianship of Gabe. If he does, the game is up. And I have to keep playing until I get my brother to safety. Until I get him out of reach of the men who can hurt him.

"I'm just tired," I say. "And still a little shook up, I guess."

He pulls me into his arms, rubs my back, holds me so close that if I'm not careful, I'll lose myself in him. I'll let myself believe in him again.

"Let's go home," he says.

The flight is uneventful. I close my eyes and pretend to sleep, not wanting to talk to anyone.

When we land in Palermo, Rafa goes his own way and when we get to the house, Stefan disappears into his study. I go up to my room and have to smile when, before I even reach it, I hear the birds chirping away inside. It's a good sound, that.

I walk in and they turn to look at me, to watch me walk toward them.

"Well, hello," I say, crouching down to put my finger

through the bars. They both come to greet me and I love this. I love their innocence. Their trust.

I open the balcony doors and take in the breeze. It's warm but I stand in it, inhale the salt air. I love it here. I love it more than I do Rome. It's the company I keep that's the problem.

After a quick shower, I head downstairs to find Miss Millie getting ready to go out.

"Where are you going?" I ask.

"Errands," she says. "It's market day and we need some things."

"Do you think I could go with you?"

"It's just errands, Gabriela."

"I don't mind. I can help. And I'd love to see the market." I don't care about any of these things, but I want to talk to her.

She softens. "Let's ask Stefan. If he doesn't mind, I'd love the company."

We both go to the study and Miss Millie knocks.

"Come in," Stefan says from inside.

He's sitting behind his desk with his laptop open. "Gabriela was wondering if she could join me at the market," Miss Millie says.

I hate having to ask his permission. It kills me. But I smile sweetly.

Stefan shifts his gaze from her to me and I expect him to say no.

"Take four extra guards and make sure Lucas is one of them."

"Four? That's overkill, isn't it?" I protest.

"Is it?" he asks. "If you want to go, you take four extra men."

I turn to Miss Millie. "If you don't mind?"

"They don't bother me," she says, and we close the door and head into town.

The market is set up on one long street a few blocks from the beach with stalls and stalls of fresh fruits and vegetables, with a variety of cheese and olives and meats, basket weavers, jewelry makers and all sorts of trinkets.

I walk with Miss Millie as the men trail us.

"Do you know Rafa's father well?" I ask her.

She tests two peaches and tells the woman at the stall how much she wants. "I've known Rafa since he was born, and although I know his father, Antonio didn't like him, which meant he didn't come to the house much."

"Why didn't he like him?"

She shrugs a shoulder as she takes the bag of peaches and puts them into her trolley then orders cherries. "He didn't think Francesco was good enough for Rafa's mother. Not that he thought anyone was."

"That's a little bit of a strange story to me. So, the three of them lived together for a time? Stefan's mom, dad and aunt?"

"Yes. Antonio met Laura through her sister. They were very close before and even after he and Laura married."

"Like..." I trail off. She turns to me and I know I should tread lightly. "Were they ever together together?"

She shakes her head. "Never. Not like that. Not that I know. I think they were just very good friends. The sisters were close, too. It was a house filled with love. Hard to imagine that sometimes. Hard to see how it all turned out."

"Miss Millie," I ask when we reach the cheese stall. "I want to ask you something important."

She turns to me. "Of course."

I glance at the soldiers and she must read what I'm thinking.

"Lucas," she calls out to one of them. He comes over. "I forgot to buy apples. Go get me a kilo please."

He nods and disappears. She turns to me, smiles and gives me a wink. "He's the only one who speaks English. Now ask me your question."

"It's about Rafa. Do you trust him?"

She studies me and I get the feeling she knows much more than she lets on. She may slip in and out of rooms like a ghost, but she hears and sees and knows.

"I believe Rafa is a good person. I believe he loves Stefan."

"But?" Because I hear that but.

"He's conflicted, Gabriela. You have to understand that he grew up at Stefan's side. They're just a few months apart in age. But he always knew he wasn't a Sabbioni. His father made sure he remembered that. Never gave him his own approval but made sure Rafa always knew he wasn't quite part of the Sabbioni family. And we're human. That breeds a certain hostility. A jealousy, maybe. Even if one is unaware of it. I don't think Rafa would willingly harm Stefan. But although they may be as close as brothers, he's no more than a soldier, even if he is on a rung above these men." She gestures to the men hovering near us.

Lucas returns a moment later. "These good, Millie?" Lucas asks, showing her the bag of apples.

She peers inside, picks one out and inspects it. "Perfect. Thank you, Lucas. I'll make my pie later."

"Can't wait," he says, and we move on.

I replay what she just said. And what she didn't say.

I have so much to process and my first priority has to be moving Gabe. The thing is, I don't have any money to do it. I can't ask my father. I can't ask Stefan. And the alternative, Rafa's offer to move him, I'm not sure I want that.

At the thought of Rafa, my father's words come echoing back.

You'll want her to hear so she doesn't go running to tell her husband the truth—the whole truth—because I think he'll murder you with his bare hands if he hears what you did to his precious wife.

The whole truth.

What is he talking about?

That breeds a certain hostility. A jealousy, maybe. Even if one is unaware of it.

Miss Millie's wrong. Rafa has already betrayed Stefan. Knowingly.

But was it remorse that after my father admitted to my mother's murder, he wanted to get me out of there? Was it guilt at his betrayal? Because Miss Millie's also right about us being human. And nothing is ever black or white. Too much gray to cloud our thoughts, our actions. It's intention that counts.

No, that's a cop out.

Intention and action, the latter at least to some extent. Even if Rafa felt guilt at betraying Stefan, he still betrayed him when he took me to my father. When he lied to him about it.

I'm glad I talked to Melanie when I was at Clear Meadows. I told her I'd try to move Gabe and that I wanted her to go with him. I remember how she looked at Rafa when I told her. Rafa who hovered at the edge of the room, a guard. A soldier. A jailor.

I know if I'd wanted to walk out of there, he wouldn't have let me go. And I think Melanie understood too. I mean, she knows who my father is. She's smart enough to know that what happened to Gabe wasn't an accident. And she promised she'd take care of him.

When we get back to the house, I help Miss Millie unpack the groceries before going upstairs to my room.

Something seems strange as I walk down the hallway, but I can't put my finger on it. A sense of dread fills me, though, and has me slowing my steps. By the time I reach my door and put my hand on the doorknob, it's sweaty and I realize what's different.

It's quiet. Too quiet.

I open the door slowly and look at the gilded cage of the lovebirds. It's quieter yet in this room. Quieter than in the hallway even with the sound of the sea below.

Because the birds aren't singing.

I see them before I even enter the room. See their pretty colors, the bright green and yellow, such happy colors.

With heavy steps I reach the cage and my hand comes to my mouth. The birds are lying on their backs. Lying like they just fell right off their small perch into a scattering of bird food littering the floor of the cage. Side by side, lovers in life. Lovers in death.

I kneel down and open the cage door to reach inside and lift Marguerite out. She's so soft and light in my palm. I pet her little head, her still chest, and feel the trickle of a tear.

"Gabriela?" Stefan says from behind me. "What are you doing?"

I turn. I didn't even hear him come.

He looks at me, at the bird in my hand, at her lover lying in the cage. He walks slowly inside, forehead creasing.

"They're dead," I say.

He shifts his gaze to mine as he stands over us. "Dead?" He takes a few moments to lean down and look around. "Maybe they were old," he says. "But..."

Maybe they were. But for them to die together? Like this? That's not natural.

"I'll get you two new birds," he says to me.

I shake my head, stand. I put Marguerite back inside the cage. "I don't want new birds."

I turn away from him and from my closet, I take a pair of shoes out of its box and return with the box to the room. I arrange the tissue paper inside, making a small nest for them, then reach into the cage to take each bird out, Marguerite and Mephistopheles. Maybe I doomed them with those names.

Placing them side by side in the box, I take one last look and place the tissue paper over them before putting on the lid.

"I'll bury them," I say to Stefan.

"We'll do it together."

I shake my head. "Can you get the cage out of here?"

"Gabriela, you don't have to do it alone—"

"I want to be alone!" I force in a breath to calm myself. "Please just get the cage out of my room."

One eye narrows but he nods, his gaze on me strange, worried maybe? But something else, too.

Maybe he's just looking at the crazy woman I've become.

"Thank you," I say and walk out of the room and he doesn't follow me as I make my way down to the cove where I dig a hole with my hands, my eyes somehow dry. I put the box inside and cover the grave. I even say a little prayer over them. Stupid, I know. They're just birds. But they were my birds. Even they couldn't escape the danger that follows me. The death.

After some time, I take out my cell phone and I call Rafa. He answers on the first ring.

"Does your offer to help me still stand?" I ask.

"Anything you need."

26

STEFAN

I move the cage to my study. My men watch Gabriela down in the cove but give her space, privacy.

The birds died together. That's not old age.

The goldsmith wasn't quite forthcoming at the start of our meeting and I knew from his behavior that something was up. He was too skittish, too anxious. But it didn't take much to buy his information. Then again, maybe he was paid to appear anxious.

I was right. Gabriel Marchese had commissioned the cage. Not my uncle. He'd told the smith what he'd wanted, given several photographs of my house. He'd even given him the piece of music for one compartment and had wanted a second, secret compartment.

He'd also had him destroy the plans once he'd paid for the cage.

My uncle wouldn't have known about the second compartment. He wouldn't have known that he'd be delivering his own confession in that gift.

He partnered with Marchese and Marchese fucked him.

Although I wonder how long they've been partners.

What I found in that second compartment was a thumb drive. I assumed the pellets inside it were just to keep it from rattling around in the little pocket. Without a thought, I'd left the food at the bottom of the cage when I'd retrieved the drive. My guess is the birds had eaten those pellets of food and died. To be sure, though, I've already sent a sample for testing.

I don't like to see Gabriela upset, don't like her to lose one more thing, even if they are just birds. But what's more important is what I found.

On that drive were photographs and voice recordings.

I know now how that second boat arrived so quickly when Gabriela turned to her father for help after Alex's murder. I wonder if that's the reason Marchese is fucking with my uncle because my uncle fucked with him.

Although I can't be sure on that. They could have been in on it together from the start. But would Marchese have given his permission for his own daughter to be left at the bottom of a well? He's an evil prick, but isn't that too far even for him?

It doesn't matter. Either way, they both fucked me.

But Marchese wanted me to learn the truth. Or at least his manipulated version of it.

When I'd asked Rafa to get Gabriela's phone set up, to add the phone numbers and make sure she had what she needed, he'd added something else. Something I wasn't aware of. He'd added spyware that could track her calls, her keystrokes, location. All of it. I'm sure her new phone has the same.

One of the voice recordings on the drive is from Rafa to his father on the night Gabriela was kidnapped telling him she was on the move and that Marchese's men were coming for her via the cove.

Now, did Rafa's father and Marchese plan the second boat together? Or was that purely my uncle's doing? Marchese wouldn't know that his conversation with his daughter had been picked up. He wouldn't know that another enemy would be out there too, once she was far enough away from land and too far for me to protect her.

In all the speculation, I am certain about three things:

Marchese is my enemy.

My uncle is my enemy.

Rafa is my enemy.

Rafa.

Christ.

The photos of him are the most damning. Overkill even. Did Marchese intend on hurting me personally somehow by showing me over and over and over again the many times Rafa betrayed me? Betrays me still.

But why?

Why would Rafa betray me? What does he have to gain by that? Is it as simple as seeking his father's approval? Christ. How pathetic if that's it.

I get up, brush my hand through my hair. I walk out of the study and to the man standing at the patio.

"Is she still down there?"

He nods. "She's on the phone with her brother is what I'm told."

My cell phone buzzes in my pocket. I take it out, swipe the green bar when I see it's Lucas, the man overseeing the surveillance of both Rafa's house and my uncle's.

"Yes?" I ask.

"Rafa's got company," Lucas says.

"Who?"

"Your cousin. Clara."

"Clara? She's in Syracuse."

"Not anymore she's not. Want us to go in?"

"No. Not yet. I'm on my way."

"Stefan, is that a good idea?" Lucas asks. He's been around a long time. Served my father before me. He knows our family. And he's warned about the Catalano family since the day of my father's death.

"It's a fine idea." My voice comes tight and short as I walk out of the house and tell one of my men to have the Bugatti brought around.

"I know that family, Stefan. I've known them longer than you. They're no good. Your father knew it, too."

I don't like that. I don't like hearing it. But maybe it's more true than I'm willing to accept.

"Thank you, Lucas. I appreciate that."

I disconnect the call and a few minutes later, I'm driving on my own to Rafa's house because I have to. I have to see for myself. Hear for myself. I have to know.

27

STEFAN

My head isn't any clearer by the time I park the car and walk up to Rafa's front door. I'm about to ring the doorbell when I hear Clara's flirty laughter coming from the back of the house. I walk around, opening the gate quietly as I do.

But it's not quiet enough. Rafa's no fool.

Before I'm two steps in, he's come around the corner, pistol in hand, his face hard.

I'm not surprised by his sudden, armed appearance. It's one of the reasons he's my right-hand man.

"Rafa," I say, seeing him with different eyes.

He uncocks the gun and tucks it into the back of his jeans. "Stefan," he starts, and I note that he is surprised. Anxious even. "What are you doing here?"

I walk toward him. I can feel how hard my expression is and I need to concentrate to keep it level.

"I wanted a drink," I say.

In the time it takes me to answer him, he's schooled his features and now gives me an easy smile. At least it's meant to look easy. Now that I'm paying attention, though, I see it's not. Not really.

"Well, then I have a surprise." We walk around the back of the property and I find Clara sitting on the patio.

"Tada!" she announces, standing, stretching her arms wide.

"Clara dropped by out of the blue," Rafa says.

"Well, this is a nice surprise," I say, kissing each of Clara's cheeks when I get to her. "Aren't you supposed to stay in Syracuse?"

"Ugh, Stefan," she starts, sitting back down and picking up her glass of wine. "Syracuse is the most boring place on earth."

"I offered to move you to Rome."

"I'd rather be here, in Palermo. With my two favorite cousins," she says, smiling up at Rafa who is still standing.

"You're alone again?" Rafa asks. His tone is so opposite Clara's light one.

I nod.

"I told you. You can't do that, Stef. There are people who..." he trails off.

"I can take care of myself, Rafa. And besides, you're here. I can trust you, can't I?"

"Don't be stupid," he says. "What can I get you to drink?"

I see he's drinking a Peroni. "Beer's fine."

He disappears into the house.

Clara sits back, taking a cigarette from what I assume is Rafa's pack and lighting one. She folds one leg over the other and studies me as she exhales smoke.

"Now that you married her, can I come back?"

"You're already back. You clearly don't need my permission."

"I was just visiting. Dropping in."

"It's quite a drive to drop in."

Rafa comes outside then, sets a bottle of beer in front of me and has a second ready for himself. He finishes the open bottle and picks up the second.

Using my wedding ring as a bottle opener, I pop the lid and drink a long swallow. I watch the two of them.

"You know what I miss," Clara begins, setting her cigarette on the ashtray and leaning forward toward me. "Us."

"Us?" I've always known Clara to be more cunning than Rafa may choose to see. It's never bothered me before. It bothers me now.

"Us," she says, standing. "Together." She reaches back to unzip her dress and a moment later, she's standing in a bikini.

I thought she'd have been naked under there and I mentally berate myself for thinking it. For thinking her so deceptive. I've known her all my life. She's family.

But then she gives me a wicked grin, reaches back to undo her top and drops it to the ground.

I look at her. At her heavy breasts with their large, dark nipples.

And she's not done yet. I wonder if she's encouraged by my silence because she hooks her thumbs into her bikini bottoms and pushes them down slowly, bending deeply as she does, giving Rafa an eyeful.

"Clara," he says, her name a command.

She cranes her neck to look at him, remaining bent over all the while.

"Yes?" she asks coyly.

"Put your clothes back on."

She turns to me, straightens, cocks her head to the side.

I slide my gaze down, down to the bare slit of her sex, to the pussy lips just visible to me.

"Do you want me to put my clothes back on, Stefan?" She turns in a circle, faces me again. "You used to prefer me like this."

I sip my beer, let my gaze slide over her once more, then meet her eyes. "That was past. Get dressed."

Her expression changes, hardens. "That sad little virgin bride of yours can't be giving you what you need."

"You don't know what I need, Clara. We had our fun, but I'm married now. Things are different."

"You were forced to marry the spoiled brat. Everyone knows that. No one would judge you."

"I could give a fuck about anyone judging me. Get dressed. You're embarrassing yourself."

Her eyes turn to slits and she looks to Rafa.

He gestures to the house. "Go inside. Close the door behind you."

She grits her teeth, bends to pick up her discarded clothes and, surprisingly, does as she's told.

Rafa watches her until the sliding glass door is closed fully.

"You fucking her again?" I ask him.

He nods once.

"Why didn't you tell me?"

"I didn't think it mattered. She shouldn't have done that."

"No, she shouldn't."

Silence falls again. Rafa picks up his second beer, drinks half of it.

"I actually came here for a reason," I say.

"I don't mind you coming just to have a beer. We used to do it a lot. I miss it."

"Me too. So much has changed. But I want to repay your father for his help in finding Gabriela. For that beautiful wedding gift which I'm sure cost a fortune."

"He doesn't expect anything. I'm sure—"

"I want to organize a dinner. You can bring Clara if you want. You should. If you're a couple, Gabriela's going to have to get used to it. And Clara's going to have to get used to Gabriela."

"We're not a couple, Stef. It's not like that."

"You're just fucking her."

"Yeah."

"Well, I'll leave it up to you." I finish my beer, stand. "Saturday. A dinner to honor your father. To show my gratitude. It's time this family came together as a family."

Rafa stands. Nods. "That's a good idea, Stefan. It's past time."

"I'll see you Saturday."

Rafa walks around the table and we look at each other for a long moment and I try to see him as he was. Because now, what I see is the face of a traitor. How sweetly they smile.

"Everything okay?" he asks.

"You're like a brother to me. You know that, don't you?" I don't know why I say it.

No, I do.

His betrayal, it wounds me. Because what I say is true. He's always been like a brother to me.

He studies me, and what I see in his eyes isn't the expression I expect. There's a deep sadness inside him.

"You *are* a brother to me, Stefan," he says. He leans in to hug me, kisses my cheek. And once again, I'm left thinking of Judas in the Garden of Gethsemane.

Of the kiss that nailed Christ to the cross.

28

GABRIELA

I step out of the shower just as my phone starts to ring the next evening. I wrap a towel around myself, check the display. It's Rafa.

Taking a deep breath in, I sit on the edge of the tub to answer.

"It's done," Rafa says.

"He's moved?"

"Yes. With the nurse you wanted."

"Where are they?"

"I'm just texting you their location. You can call her to confirm."

"I will," I say. I'd feel better if Rafa had given me the money to do it myself, but he wouldn't do that. Said he'd take care of the transfer. That I had to trust him. I just hope I'm not wrong about this because if I am, Gabe will be the one to pay.

"If you need anything else—"

"I'm trusting you. I probably shouldn't."

I hear him sigh. "I understand that you don't trust me.

But hearing your father and you talk, fuck, Gabriela, I shouldn't have taken you to him. I shouldn't—"

"He told me the truth, at least."

"Only to hurt you."

"No. Well, that too, probably. But that's not all. He's losing to Stefan and he'll do whatever he needs to do, hurt whomever he needs to hurt, to change that."

"Fathers are...difficult."

"Understatement."

"Your brother's safe at least."

"You won't tell Stefan where he is?"

"No."

"You won't tell anyone else?"

"No. I swear it."

"Why are you helping me, Rafa?"

"I don't know. This whole thing is a fucking shit show. It's not what I wanted. Not how I wanted it."

"What do you mean?"

Silence. "It's complicated."

"The birds died," I say out of the blue.

"What?"

"The birds in the cage. They were both dead when I came into my room yesterday."

"Both?"

I nod even though I know he can't see me.

"I'm sorry."

"Do you think Stefan...I mean, I don't understand anymore. I can't wrap my head around any of this."

"I don't think Stefan did anything to your birds, Gabriela."

I know it's stupid to even think it. I mean, why would he? How would he?

"What are you going to do now?" Rafa asks, interrupting my thoughts.

"What can I do? I have no money. I'm in Sicily in a heavily guarded house and I'm married to the man who holds the keys. And if that's not enough, I'm trusting the man who is betraying his best friend."

"That friend is your jailor," Rafa says.

But it doesn't feel right. I can't just forget the tender moments. The good things Stefan has done. The way he's cared for me.

"You just promise me, Rafa, please, that you'll keep Gabe safe."

"You have my word."

I hear the bedroom door open and I startle.

"Gabriela?" it's Stefan.

"Just a minute," I call out. "I have to go," I whisper to Rafa.

"Let me know if you need anything else."

I disconnect the call, take a moment to calm myself before opening the door.

Stefan is at the balcony doors. "Why did you close these?" he asks. They stand open now.

"No reason."

He looks me over and I tuck the towel closer. "Have a drink with me before dinner."

"Dinner already?" I ask, simultaneously looking at the clock to find it's almost eight. I'm trying to avoid the drink invitation because I'm having a hard time looking at him.

He raises his eyebrows.

"I'm not actually hungry," I say.

"A drink first. That'll get your appetite going."

"Why?"

"Why will it get your appetite going?"

"Why do we need to have a drink."

"Because we need to talk."

"About what?"

"Christ." He walks back to the still open bedroom door and pushes it closed. "I'm trying to be civilized," he says, stalking toward me.

"A civilized mobster."

His face hardens.

"I don't want to have a drink with you."

"That's too bad."

I step backward, turning to go into the closet to put on a dress.

"No," he says, catching my arm.

"Let me go. I'll get dressed."

"No."

"Fine. Christ. You want a drink? I'll have a drink."

"What happened, Gabriela?" he asks.

"Nothing. Let me go. I'll get dressed."

"No," he says, tugging me toward him, looking down at where I'm clutching the towel. "Drop it."

"Why?"

"You told me you wanted to trust me. Trust me."

I don't move. So much has happened since I said that. Too much.

"Or do your wants change with the wind? I don't believe that. I think you're too complicated for that."

"Leave me alone, Stefan."

"No, Gabriela."

"What do you want from me?"

He comes closer still. Taking my face in his hands, he makes me look at him. "I want all of you."

I'm taken aback, trying to make sense of his words. I don't move when he undoes the towel and it drops to the floor. I watch him, try to understand the scope of emotion in his hazel eyes.

He walks backward to the bed, taking me with him. He sits on the edge of it, pulls me to stand between his legs.

From here I can already see the outline of his erection and my body responds.

"You know what the problem is?"

"There's no problem. I—"

"Problem is you don't yet know that you're mine," he pauses, letting me take in his words. His meaning. "You need to be fucked before we can talk. You need to know it. Feel it. It's the only way you'll hear me."

He traps me with his thighs as he releases my wrists to pull off his T-shirt and undo his belt. His jeans. He doesn't take himself out yet though. Just sits there like that and I look at him, at all that muscle and power and man.

And I want him.

He softens his hold on me, starts to run the tips of his fingers over the insides of my arms, leaving goosebumps in his wake. His touch is so gentle, so light and soft, so opposite who he is and all the while, he watches me and I watch him, and he's right. Maybe I'm stupid but he's right. I do want to trust him. And more than that. I want him, too. I want all of him.

"There's something wrong with me," I say.

"There's nothing wrong with you. You've just been mistreated. But I see you, Gabriela. I *see* you. And I won't hurt you."

I tug to free myself. This is too much. He's too much.

He pulls me down onto his lap, one hand cupping the back of my head and bringing me to him to kiss me.

I don't kiss him back, twisting to free myself instead, but he easily keeps hold of me. I'm straddling him, my legs wide. He slides one hand between them, and my body prepares to betray me.

"I can't do this." I have to protect myself. I can't give myself to him. Hasn't he proven that?

He tugs my head backward, his fingers working, his mouth on my throat, on my mouth. It's like my body goes into auto-pilot when he touches me. Like I have no control over it. Like he owns it.

Isn't that what he's saying though? That he owns me?

"Stefan."

He pulls back, and his eyes are dark when I look at them and I forget what I want to say. What I was trying to say.

It's like he knows it and he grins. A moment later we're on our knees and he's still holding me, one hand in my hair, the other cupping my sex.

"Take me out," he says.

I lick my lips, my gaze dropping to the bulge in his pants. My hands move without my brain's permission and I take him out, cupping his cock like it's the Holy Grail. I feel the smooth length of it, smear pre-cum in my palm as I lick my lips again and return my gaze to his.

He watches me and a moment later, I feel pressure on the back of my head as he guides me down to him and I take the steel rod of his cock in my mouth and I'm greedy when it comes to this.

He moans as he moves me along his length and when he pulls me off, there's a pop when the suction is broken. His eyes are black when he brings my face to his and kisses me before turning me so I'm facing away from him. He pulls me into him, and my back is against his front. One of his hands is between my legs and the other is kneading a nipple while he trails kisses along my neck, my throat.

He pushes me forward, down on my belly and his hands

move to my hips. He lifts them, tilts my hips upward and I look back to look at him look at me as he spreads me open. Eyes on mine, he slides all the way inside me, stretching me, seating himself fully.

I'm unprepared. I make a sound of protest, his cock too big, my passage too tight. But when I try to move, he holds me down.

"Are you scared?" he asks, cock still buried inside me.

I shake my head.

"Because you trust me not to hurt you."

Trust.

Is it true what he says? Do I trust him? On some level, I do. Or I want to. But do I have any choice?

What I feel though, the fact that I'm not scared he'll hurt me, that's not a choice. It's what I know.

But then he draws out slowly and slides his cock up to my other hole.

"Stefan, no. You're too big. I can't—"

"Shh. Trust me. I told you I won't hurt you."

"I—"

"You're going to give me this. And you're going to know that you're mine. And I don't hurt what's mine."

One hand slides around to my clit and as he closes his fingers around it he pushes against the tight ring. I feel him, his big cock lubricated with my juices. It's slippery and as he plays with my clit, I open to him and even though it hurts, I want this. I want him to have me like this.

He moves slowly, carefully, all the while playing with me, talking to me and feeling him like this, inside me there. It's different, intense. Like all the sensations are multiplied by a thousand. There's pain and pleasure and they take turns, one giving way to the other, again and again and I come more than once before he's fully inside me and all I can do is feel. Like I become sensation and it's just him and me and us like this. Close. So close.

Stefan inside me.

Stefan closer than ever inside me and maybe it's that I want to forget. Maybe it's my escape, however momentary, but I give myself over to it. My body relaxes and I just feel and trust and when he's fully in me, I hear him, hear his breathing shorten, feel him thicken even more and he's saying my name too, telling me I'm beautiful. Telling me I'm his.

And when he begins to fuck me, I lose all conscious thought.

I am a ball of nerves. Of pleasure. Of us.

I don't know where one orgasm ends and the other begins. I don't know where he ends, and I begin.

And when he stills inside me and I feel him filling me up, I squeeze around him, and I want more of him. All of him. Every part of him.

It's all I can think as I go limp and my vision goes dark. And his name on my lips is all I hear.

I don't feel him slide out of me.

I don't feel him lift me up and carry me to the bed.

When I open my eyes, it's like I'm floating and he's there and smiling and he cleans me so gently, so tenderly before tucking me into bed.

And I just lie there, spent.

When he's dressed, he sits on the edge of the bed and smiles down at me, brushes hair gently back from my face.

"Now you're mine. Every part of you."

How does he look the way he does? Didn't what we just did cost him as much as it did me? He seems the opposite of me. Revitalized.

He leans down to kiss my mouth.

"Get dressed when you're ready. Come downstairs. We'll have that drink before dinner."

I turn my head to watch him walk to the door.

He stops there, looks back at me and I must be a sight because he just grins and walks out the door.

29

GABRIELA

It takes me a little time to get up and I decide to shower again. Cold this time. It does the trick, waking me up. By the time I get downstairs it's a good half hour later.

Stefan is sitting outside watching the dark blue water. He turns when he hears me and without a word, I take my place opposite him at the table and when I sit down, I can still feel him inside me, feel what we did.

He just watches me, drinking his whiskey.

"Okay?" he asks.

I nod, a little embarrassed. Something is different with us.

Without asking if I want it, he pours me a glass of white wine.

I pick it up, taking the first sip. I savor it, needing it.

Being with him like we were, it fucks with me. Makes me go all soft.

I drink another swallow of wine.

"I like how you look after being fucked."

"How do I look?"

"Soft. Dreamy."

"It's your magical cock, I guess."

"Probably," he winks and his expression is disarming. "But what I like more is how you look at me after."

I don't need to ask what he means. This one I know. I look at him like he's a god. My god.

"It's just sex."

"No, it's not. And you know it."

I do.

But I have to make myself remember. Remember New York. Remember Gabe. Remember what my father told me.

That's the one that does it. That wipes that dreamy expression off my face. And he sees it instantly.

"You're ready to talk," he says. It's not a question and if I didn't know better, I'd say he looks a little disappointed.

"Tell me what happened between the morning we were in New York and that afternoon? Tell me what has you thinking you need to hate me again."

"I do hate you, Stefan. I never stopped hating you."

"We both know that's not true."

"You want to argue it? Argue how I feel versus how you think I feel?"

"No, I don't. I think it'd be a boring conversation. Truce, Gabriela."

"Why?"

"Because whether you want to admit it or not, we have a common enemy and you and I are one another's only allies."

"Enemies and allies. I've never heard those words so much before meeting you."

"Explain to me again how you got a bump on the back of your head during the car chase."

"I bumped it against the window. I told you."

"Do you see how that doesn't make physical sense to me?"

"It all happened so fast. Maybe I hit it against something else. I don't know, Stefan."

He studies me, eyes narrowing. "You were right," he says.

"Right about what?" Is he letting it go?

"Rafa and Clara. They're together."

"How do you know that?"

"I went to Rafa's house yesterday. She was there and Rafa confirmed it."

"I don't care. Why do you think I would care?"

"Just thought I'd share it with you. I'll share more. Those men Rafa thought were following you the other day, they were my men."

"What? Why? I mean, I didn't even see anyone. I couldn't figure out who was chasing us."

He remains silent while I try to work through this.

"Why did you have men following us?"

"I had them following Rafa. Not you. I wanted to be sure you were safe, and I had doubts about Rafa. Doubts that have been confirmed."

"What?"

I feel my forehead crease as I think about Gabe. About where he is. Where Rafa said he put him. When I tried to call Melanie to make sure they were okay, I only got voice mail.

"The birds were poisoned, Gabriela."

"Poisoned? Why? Who would do that? How?"

He reaches into his pocket and pulls something out. He sets it on the table. It's a thumb drive.

"I don't understand."

"I went to see the man who made the cage when we were in New York. To be honest, that was the reason I needed to go. But I'm glad I was able to take you to see your brother."

I hear the last part but set it aside for now. "It was made in New York?"

Stefan nods.

I'm not surprised, am I? My father had it made. Does Stefan know that?

"I recognized the name of the smith. And the reason I looked into it is there's no way my uncle could afford to gift something like that. Not on his own."

"My father paid for it," I say.

He studies me.

I study him.

"This was inside it." He gestures to the drive.

"Where?"

"In a secret compartment. There were food pellets in the compartment too. I'd thought they were just buffer and didn't think twice about what got left on the bird cage floor."

"I'm not following."

"I had the pellets tested. They were poisoned."

"Why? Why would someone poison birds? Why would my father? And why would he, and I assume it was him, why would he hide a thumb drive in our wedding gift?"

"Kill two birds with one stone. One pellet, I guess."

"That's not funny."

"I'm not being funny."

"What's on the drive?"

"Betrayal. Rafa's. My uncle's. He's the one who had you kidnapped. Rafa's the one who told him your father was sending men to pick you up."

My blood turns to ice and I shudder. "How would he know?"

"He had spyware on your cellphone. He's probably heard and read everything."

"But why would he do that to me?"

"I'd bet Catalano is behind Alex's murder," Stefan says, not answering my question.

"But why, Stefan?"

"To keep us apart? To hurt you? To plant an enemy in my house? What better for him to do that than to have an ally in my own bed."

"I want to see what's on that drive."

"That's fine. I'll show you."

He stands and I do too, and I follow him into his study. He has me sit in his chair as he loads the thumb drive into the computer. He lets me work my way through the files. The photos. The recordings. All of it.

And I feel sick.

"Oh God."

"It's all right. I'm taking care of it."

I shake my head, look up at him. "You don't understand."

"What don't I understand?"

"I made a mistake."

His eyebrows furrow together.

"I saw my father," I start, my voice unsteady. "Rafa took me there before he took me to see my brother. That's where we were."

Stefan's face hardens.

"The bump on my head...when I tried to get out of the car, when I figured out where he was taking me, he knocked me out."

"Rafa *hit* you?" he asks through gritted teeth.

"It's not...I think..."

"He. Hit. You."

He turns to the door, hands fisted.

I stand, grab hold of his arm.

"No, Stefan. I think he was desperate. Confused even."

He spins to face me.

"He. Hit. You. Why are you making excuses for him?"

I think about Rafa at my father's house. I think about what he said, what I saw, that remorse, that sadness.

But that's not important right now.

"My father told me why you did it. Why you wanted custody of Gabe."

"Your father is a master manipulator."

"He told me he cut me off. That he'd left it all to Gabe. And that's why you wanted him. That's why you wouldn't let me put my name down as guardian."

He doesn't say a word.

"It's true, isn't it?"

It takes him a moment, but he nods once.

"I need to call my brother, Stefan."

When I try to scoot around him, he grabs hold of me. "He's fine. Your brother's fine."

I shake my head. "He's not. He's...oh God. You don't understand."

"What have you done, Gabriela?"

I turn my face up to his. "Rafa moved him. Just yesterday. He moved Gabe and Melanie to a secret location. Out of my father's reach. Out of yours."

Stefan's forehead wrinkles as he tries to make sense of what I'm saying. "You went to him for help." It's not a question. And I'm not sure it's anger I feel from him. Betrayal maybe.

I betrayed him.

"I don't know who to trust, Stefan. I keep making mistakes. And others keep paying for those mistakes. Everywhere I turn, I have enemies."

He takes my arms, shakes me violently. "I'm not one of those enemies! When will you see that? When will you believe it?"

My eyes burn with unshed tears.

"Tell me. Tell me why you want Gabe. Say it yourself. Then tell me how you're not my enemy. I mean, I've signed the papers. You don't need me. I'm no use to you now. I have no value anymore. I'm not precious. I never was." I mutter the last words under my breath and I don't think he hears but, but when I see his face, I know I'm wrong.

Because Stefan stops.

And he just watches me for the longest time and his expression is so strange.

"You're wrong. So wrong." He releases me, steps away and runs a hand through his hair. "Fuck." He shakes his head. "And you and I may be the last to see it." He shifts his gaze away momentarily. "I am a fool."

"What?"

"You are the most precious of pawns. Don't you see?"

"I don't understand."

"And everyone knows it. I've underestimated my enemies."

"Stefan?"

He turns to me. "You still don't see."

I'm confused.

"I care about you, Gabriela. You are precious to me. And they all know it."

What?

He shifts his gaze, exhales like he's just understood something. He looks at me again. "Hurting you hurts me. Rafa was right. He saw long before anyone else. You're my weakness. And they'll keep hurting you to hurt me."

I don't hear his words, though. They're noise. White noise. I'm still trying to process what he just said.

Precious.

I'm precious to him.

Stefan takes his phone out of his pocket. "Where's your brother?"

I look up at him and wonder if he realizes it. If he realizes what he just said. "I have the location on my phone. Rafa texted it to me."

"Go get it."

I hurry out of the study and up to my bedroom. I grab my phone, run back down to the study to find two soldiers inside with Stefan. He's giving them orders. I recognize the one. Lucas from the market.

"Here," I say, handing my phone to Stefan.

He takes it, reads the address, sits down behind his desk to type it into his computer.

"Call him," he tells me without looking up.

But I don't get a chance to because the sound of men's raised voices coming from the front entrance of the house has us both up. Has Stefan drawing a weapon from a desk drawer as he pushes me behind him.

"Stay," he commands, and opens the study door.

The moment he does, I hear a curse, a grunt, followed by more yelling and footsteps and a moment later, Rafa appears at the open study door where Stefan stands waiting, each man with a weapon in hand. Each looking as murderous as the other.

30

STEFAN

"You love me like a fucking brother, but I have to fight my fucking way in?" Rafa roars. He stumbles when he comes toward me.

I catch him, right him, uncock my gun, and shove it into the back waistband of my jeans.

"What are you doing here, Rafa?"

He looks at me, looks beyond me and into the study.

Gabriela steps beside me and I watch his gaze follow her.

"I wanted a drink," Rafa says finally.

"Looks to me like you've had plenty to drink already. Give me that." I gesture to the pistol in his hand.

He looks down at it like he forgot it was there. A moment later, he shoves it into the back of his jeans and walks past me into the study. He pours himself two fingers of whiskey and swallows it at once before refilling his glass and dropping down into a seat on the couch. His movement is so clumsy that some of the whiskey splashes over his hand.

"Go upstairs, Gabriela," I tell her without turning around.

"Not until I know my bro—"

"Now." I look at her and give a subtle shake of my head.

She looks from me to Rafa.

"I said go. Now," I repeat.

"Let her stay," Rafa says.

I turn to him. "Give me your gun, Rafa."

"Why? What do you think I'm going to do?"

"You're drunk. You just barged into my house drunk and brandishing a gun."

"Don't you trust me?"

"Give me your gun. I won't ask again."

He stands, reaches back.

I step in front of Gabriela and I'm pretty sure he notices because he gives a shake of his head, pulls the gun out of its place and sets it on the corner of my desk. I pick it up, take the cartridge out and shove it in my pocket.

"Satisfied?" he asks.

"Why are you here?"

"Because Clara snores," he says with a chuckle as he downs his next glass of whiskey. "But you know that."

I don't turn to Gabriela but wait for Rafa to pour himself yet another glass before facing me.

He studies me, then Gabriela. He cocks his head to the side as he sips his drink.

I shift my gaze to Gabriela. "Go upstairs," I tell her again.

"I said let her stay," Rafa intervenes.

"But you don't give the orders," I remind him.

"Maybe I should," he counters, taking a step toward me.

I take one to match his. "Be careful, cousin."

He snorts, looks again to Gabriela, lets his gaze roam over her.

"That's my *wife*," I remind him.

"You used to be more generous."

"What the fuck does that mean?"

Rafa meets my gaze head on. "It means you used to share." He shifts his gaze to her and when he takes a step toward her, something primitive inside me takes over. Rage boils in my gut.

Mine.

It's the single thought in my mind.

"You're getting soft, Stef," Rafa says. "She's making you soft. Weak." He lifts his hand and I make fists with mine as my entire body vibrates with energy.

When he runs the backs of his knuckles over her cheek, Gabriela's arm comes flying to slap his face, but he catches her wrist in the same instant I catch his.

"Remove. Your. Hand." My voice is low, calm, opposite the rage burning inside me.

"You should share her," Rafa says.

"And you should know better."

But he's drunk.

"Like we used to. Then we'll be like brothers again."

"Remove your hand or I'll break it."

Rafa looks at me, searches my face and something overrides his drunken, reckless stupidity because he lets her go. "No doubt," he says.

I see his handprint on her soft flesh, see how small her wrist is, know how easily it can be broken. How easily men like us can break her.

"Lucas." I haven't yet let go of Rafa's arm and I don't raise my voice because Lucas is standing just outside the door.

"Sir." He's got his eyes on Rafa, one hand on the butt of his pistol in its holster underneath his jacket.

"Take my wife upstairs and make sure she stays there."

"I don't want—"

I turn to Gabriela. "I don't care what you want. Take your phone and make that call while I talk with my cousin."

"Mrs. Sabbioni," Lucas says, standing beside us.

Gabriela gives Rafa one more hard look, grabs her phone and exits the room.

Lucas closes the door.

After a moment, I release Rafa.

"Fuck," he mutters, walking away, dropping again into a seat on the sofa and running fingers through his messy hair.

"What the fuck do you think you're doing?" I ask. I should kill him. Here and now. What I saw on that drive is all the evidence I need of his betrayal. But I can't do it. I can't. "What is going on with you? I could kill you, you know that?"

"It's all going to hell, Stefan. Has been ever since you brought her here."

"Gabriela has nothing to do with whatever's going on with you. Now tell me what it is before I lose my temper."

"And what? Break my arms? My legs?"

"You took her to her father. To my enemy. I'd be in my right to do both of those things."

He grits his teeth, lifting his head, then turning it away. "You don't understand."

"Then explain to me why you lied to me. Why you took my wife to my enemy. To *her* enemy. And have no doubt he is that."

"He's her father, Stefan."

"And?"

"Family's important. You've always taken your father for granted." His words are slurred and slow, like it's taking effort to string them together.

"My father is dead because of that man. My brother is dead because of that man. Gabriela's mother is dead because of that man and her brother, well, you know well enough about him."

He drops his head, shakes it. "I need another drink." When he stands, I grab his arm to stop him.

"You've had enough."

"Not enough," he doesn't fight me, though. The opposite, at least momentarily before he gets a strange second wind. "You know what I wish, Stefan?"

When he pauses, I wait, noting the crazed look in his eyes. The look of a desperate man. Of one who's run out of options.

"I wish things could go back to the way they were. The way *we* were."

"Then be the man you were. Be my brother. Not my enemy."

"I am your brother. I'll always be that." He seems more steady on his feet as he walks to the liquor cabinet and pours himself another whiskey. He remains standing. "Do you know why my father hates me?"

"He doesn't hate you."

"Yeah, he does. You don't have to pretend. But do you know why?"

I go to him and put a hand on his shoulder. "Rafa—"

He knocks my hand off. "Do you fucking know?" he snaps, his tone biting. Like he, too, is raging.

"Why don't you tell me since it seems like you know."

He shakes his head. "They're divided, Stefan. The family. Right down the middle. Well, almost."

He means the supporting families, cousins from different regions of Sicily. My uncle in Rome, he's the only one I trust fully. "That's nothing new. It's been that way since Antonio's betrayal."

"Some don't believe you have the right to rule."

"Is your father leading that thinking?" I shouldn't do it, I know. I shouldn't bait him. I can't talk to him now. Like this. I need him sober.

He smirks, swallows more whiskey. "It should have been Antonio."

"Antonio's dead."

"He's also a traitor yet you buried his body beside the man he betrayed."

"And you know why he betrayed him. You're one of the few who does."

"In our family, conscience isn't a redeeming quality. The opposite." He picks up the bottle and drinks straight from it.

Rafa and I are the only two who know why Antonio betrayed our father. Although maybe that's not true anymore. Would the cousins have supported my father if they knew why he partnered with Marchese? If they knew that he was adding flesh trade to the family's resume?

Rafa's right about conscience. Antonio had too much of it. He found out about the deal. Knew my father's role in it. He tried to stop him, but it was too late. The women had been supplied. In the container already. On their way.

Knowing my brother, no way he could stomach being part of that. Allowing it to happen at all. That's when he went to the feds. That's when he was taken into protective custody and my father arrested. I guess he thought he could save those women and girls.

But they didn't have anything on Marchese because Marchese got rid of the container.

This is what Gabriela doesn't know. What I don't want her to know about her father.

He had it dropped off the ship. A phone call was all it took, and the captain did as he was told and dropped the container and those people vanished. No evidence. No bodies. No crime. Just a container at the bottom of the ocean.

Unless my father talked. Unless he shared his evidence.

So Marchese took care of that.

He didn't do a thorough enough job searching for the evidence though and it's in my possession now. It's what got him to hand over his daughter. Funny what hearing yourself give the order to kill a dozen women and girls sounds like when it's played back.

But I didn't find it before he found Antonio. And he took care of him too. No loose ends. I do understand that.

"Tell me what you did, Rafa," I ask, forcing myself into the present.

He looks at me and I hate what I see in his eyes.

"You know what I think?" he asks, avoiding my question, stumbling when he takes a step away. With the bottle in his unsteady hand, he points a finger at me. "I personally think you should rule. But it's not up to me. I'm like her. A fucking pawn. That's why I helped her. That's why I hid her brother when she asked me to. And now I'm here to warn you because that's how fucked up I am."

"Warn me about what?"

He drinks the last of the bottle. "Antonio wasn't like us. He wasn't ruthless. And it got him killed. If you want to survive in our world, you have to be ruthless. You can't have any weakness. You should send her away. It's best for her and you know it."

"Warn me about what?" I double back.

He looks at me, scrubs his face with both hands. "I'm tired, man."

I go to him, take him by the shoulders. "Warn me about what, Rafa?"

He studies me, and I think for a moment maybe I'm mistaken. Maybe he's not as drunk as I thought.

"I'm a traitor too, Stefan. Can't seem to make up my fucking mind which side I'm on."

I grit my teeth, give him a shake. "Rafa. Warn me about what?"

He shoves my arms away, sits down on the sofa, lays his head back. "The other families." He stares up at the ceiling. "You were right about my father. And I helped him."

I watch him, hear him.

He sets his elbows on his knees and leans into his hands, rubs his face.

"Helped him how?"

"Gabriela. The kidnapping. They would have raped—"

"I will kill you!" I roar, tugging him to his feet.

"You should," he says. He doesn't fight me. Puts up no resistance at all. And when I release him, he falls back onto the couch.

"I never wanted her hurt. You should let her go before they decide."

"Before who decides what?" I'm losing my patience.

He stands, shakes his head, shoves past me to the door. "I shouldn't be here."

I stop him, shove him into the wall. "Before. Who. Decides. What?"

"It's too late, Stefan. I came too late. Decided too fucking late. Don't you see? They're meeting now. My father has their support. He called for a vote."

Rage.

"Where?"

"They'll kill you if you go. You should take Gabriela. Take what you can. Disappear."

"I'm not a fucking coward and I have no plan to disappear. Are they meeting in Taormina?"

He shakes his head. "Catania. At the warehouse."

I look at him, shake my head, let him go and open the door. "Lucas!"

Lucas is at the door a moment later. "Get men together. We're going to Catania."

"Now?"

"Fucking now." I turn to Rafa. "My cousin will be staying here until I return."

With a signal, two soldiers enter the study as I walk out.

"Stefan!" Rafa calls out.

I don't stop. I don't look back.

"They'll kill you if you walk in there. Don't be fucking stupid."

I stop, walk back into the study to find the two soldiers restraining Rafa. Without a moment's hesitation, I draw my arm back and punch him across the jaw.

"Thanks for the warning," I say, feeling the sting of the hit as I watch his split lip bleed. "We'll talk when I'm back. I'll decide how you die then."

31

GABRIELA

"Stefan?" I call out from the top of the stairs. The soldier Lucas assigned to keep me in my room unhands me on Stefan's signal and I run down the stairs. "What's happening? Where's Rafa?"

He takes my arms and studies me for a long moment. "I need to go to Catania."

"Now? It's late."

"Did you talk to your brother?"

I shake my head. "He was asleep, but I talked to Melanie. They're fine. Safe. In a house upstate."

"Good. Go pack what you need. You'll go to them. Tonight."

"Tonight?"

"I'll make some calls on my way to Taormina and Paulo will be in touch with you soon."

"Paulo?"

"Just a back-up plan, Gabriela. Until everything's settled."

I feel the color drain from my face. "You mean you may not come back." I don't ask it as a question.

He looks at me like he's memorizing me, and I touch his face, pull him to me.

"Come with me, Stefan." I hug him tight, but I can't get close enough. I feel him slipping away. Slipping right through my fingers.

"I need to go," he says.

When he pulls back, he cups my face, wipes tears with his thumbs.

"Don't leave me alone, Stefan."

His hands tighten a little and his eyes are intense. On fire. "I have no intention of leaving you alone. I love you, Gabriela. There's nothing more precious to me than you. I love you."

I have no words. I can't find them. I just feel all the emotion bubbling up in my throat and he must see it because he hugs me to him, and I'm desperate to hold on to him. Desperate to keep him. To never let him go.

"Paulo will take care of everything until I'm back. You're to trust him. Only him."

"Please don't go. Just don't. Come with me."

He pulls back. "I can't do that. Get what you need. Just what you need. But hurry." He breaks free, signals to a soldier who takes my arms and holds me back as Stefan walks away.

"Stefan!"

"I won't leave you alone," he says, giving me one more long look. "I promise."

But he's promised before.

He's sworn.

32

STEFAN

I call Paulo and make arrangements for Gabriela as we drive to the warehouse in Catania. He'll move her brother, the nurse and Gabriela to a secret location and, if things don't go as planned for me, he'll make sure she's taken care of.

Francesco Catalano called a vote. But there's nothing to vote on. I'm Antonio Sabbioni's second son. By blood, taking over the family is my right.

Catalano himself isn't blood. They won't accept him as a leader.

The men he'll meet with are blood, but distant. No clear man in line to rule. Cousins would have to battle cousins. The closest would be Rafa and that link is not through my father.

I go over my conversation with Rafa, taking into consideration the fact that he was drunk. He never did tell me why he thinks his father hates him. He called himself a pawn. Did Catalano use him to spy on me, to betray me, with the promise of his affection? Would Rafa really fall for that? Want that?

I knew the family would not take kindly to my putting Antonio's body in the family plot. He was a traitor, it's true. But I don't regret what I did. He was still my brother.

This Marchese vendetta, it's taken my focus from the family to personal vengeance. In their eyes, I should have killed Gabriel Marchese long ago. No need to take his daughter like I did. Except that in addition to the vengeance I am owed, it would grow our territory in New York, just like my father had intended. He'd just gone about it the wrong way. What he'd agreed to I wouldn't. Ever.

I realize Gabriela hasn't asked me what I have on her father since I first took her. I understand why she doesn't. She knows it's bad. One can only tolerate so much truth.

But it's not time to think about this. Think about her. If I'm distracted, I'll fail. And if I fail, then I won't be able to keep my promise to her. And I have no intention of breaking any more promises where she's concerned.

The drive to Catania is shorter than that to Taormina. I have two dozen men with me. I hope not to need them. They don't expect me to come, but still.

"I'm a traitor too, Stefan. Can't seem to make up my fucking mind which side I'm on."

That's the thing that worries me. Which side is Rafa on because taking a vote would be moot if I were dead.

I think about the other thing he said about being a pawn. To his father, I assume. Does Catalano think the families would accept Rafa as their ruler? He's a stupid fuck if he does. Blood matters. It matters the most.

A walkie talkie screeches and Lucas pushes the button to reply.

"We're in position. There's two on the roof, two at the door. Can't get inside without making some noise."

I take the walkie talkie. "No noise. I want to be inside. I

want to see their faces and hear their lies. Once we're in, give me fifteen minutes. If you don't have a signal from me, find your way in making as much noise as you need to and kill every bastard in the place."

"You sure?" Lucas asks.

"This meeting isn't sanctioned. We'll walk in through the front door."

"That's not wise, Stefan. Let me send men to take—"

"We're walking in using the front door."

Although reluctantly, he nods.

I count the men as our remaining three SUVs pull into the parking lot.

"Just the four outside. It's not a lot," Lucas says.

"They don't expect me to show up. That's Catalano's car. And there are the cousins from Syracuse. No representation from Rome." That's a good thing.

The front doors open as the SUV I'm riding in pulls to a stop. Two soldiers, each with a machine gun slung over his shoulder, step outside and watch as I climb out. Catalano's men. Overkill with him. Always.

Tonight, we'll test their loyalty to a man sentenced to die. Because Catalano will die tonight.

"Gentlemen," I say, walking right up to them. Lucas flanks me as do two more soldiers. "Step aside."

One of Catalano's soldiers keeps his hard gaze on me but the second falters.

I take another step right up to the one with the hard eyes. "I said step aside."

"This is a private meeting, Mr. Sabbioni."

My lips move into a sneer. Who the fuck does this idiot think he is?

"Is it?" I ask, gripping his machine gun with both hands. Before he or anyone can react, I tug backward and slam the gun into his forehead, sending him stumbling, catching him with the tether. "This is my warehouse."

Footsteps from behind him have me stop as lights blink on. I count more men. Maybe half a dozen. All heavily armed.

"Stefan," Francesco Catalano calls out. He's flanked by two soldiers when he stops, looks at me, cocks his head to the side.

"Good you're here. Saves us a trip to Palermo," he says.

"Uncle." Hate makes the word sound ugly. Without taking my eyes off my uncle, I draw the machine gun back once more and knock the soldier harder this time and when he stumbles to the floor, I let him drop.

"That was unnecessary," Catalano says as the soldier scrambles back to his feet. "Hand over your weapons and come in."

"Are you inviting me into my own warehouse?"

"Don't make this ugly, Stefan."

"Oh, I'm going to make this very ugly."

"No weapons in the meeting. It was agreed upon."

"I didn't sanction a meeting. I agree to nothing."

"Things have escalated beyond your control." He gives a nod and more men step out of the shadows. We're outnumbered, easily, and out-gunned by the size of their automatic weapons.

But I've never needed that much muscle to get my point across.

The man I just knocked over takes my arms, twists them behind my back, another begins to search me. They do the same to Lucas and machine guns are aimed on the rest of my men.

"Drop your weapons," Catalano commands.

33
———
GABRIELA

When Stefan leaves, the soldier takes my arm to walk me upstairs, but I yank it away.

"Don't touch me. Don't ever touch me!"

He steps backward and I look at the closed study door. Is Rafa still here? What did he tell Stefan?

I walk toward it, but the soldier approaches. He doesn't expect me to stop, to turn to him.

"Mr. Sabbioni said you're to pack," he says.

"I will," I tell him. "I need to see Rafa first."

"I don't think—"

I don't wait for him to finish but open the study door and enter to find Rafa sitting on the couch, two soldiers standing nearby.

He looks at me when I enter and again, I see what I've glimpsed more than once in his eyes. A regret. A deep sadness.

"I'm sorry," he says to me. "I don't know what I was thinking touching you like that." He runs his hands through his hair. "Fuck."

"Leave us alone," I tell the soldiers.

They look at me and I'm not sure if they don't understand English so I repeat my command in Italian.

Rafa seems surprised by this, as do the two men, but a moment later, we're alone.

I sit on the couch.

"Aren't you afraid of me?" he asks.

"No. I'm not. Not even a little."

"He's going to get himself killed." He gets to his feet. "I need to go after him."

"Where did he go? What did you tell him?"

He shakes his head, considers, then looks at me. "There's a meeting. My father—Francesco Catalano—called it. They're voting to remove Stefan from his position."

I'm confused. Is that how this works?

When I don't speak, Rafa continues, clarifying. "They'll kill him, Gabriela."

"And you let him go? Let him walk into that trap?"

"No. I came to warn him. I should have known he'd go himself, though. He's just stubborn enough. You need to get out of here. They'll come for you. For everyone in this house."

"Does that include you?"

He looks up at the ceiling, shakes his head, then turns to me. "If I can get out of here, I can stop it."

"Why are they doing this?"

"Power. Hate. You name it. Any ugliness you can think. I need to get to him, Gabriela. They'll kill him. He doesn't understand. Doesn't know everything."

"What doesn't he understand? What doesn't he know?"

He walks to the desk, opens a drawer, then another.

"What are you doing? You can't go through Stefan's desk."

He finds what he's looking for, a pistol, and, I assume,

ammunition he pockets. "I need to go." He looks at me, gets a strange look on his face as he approaches me. "I'm sorry, Gabriela," he says, grabbing hold of me and whirling me around so my back is to his chest, the gun at my temple.

"Rafa!"

He opens the door and steps out, holding me as a shield as Stefan's soldiers draw their weapons but stand impotently watching as Rafa cocks the gun.

"I'll kill her. I'll fucking kill her! And he'll kill you if that happens."

"Let me go!" I scream, scratching my nails into his forearm trying to pull him off as he drags me to the front door, and out of it, to the side of the house. More soldiers follow, drawing weapons, orders being yelled to halt, to not shoot as long as he has me.

A few moments later, we near a building I've not been inside and Rafa pushes the door open, forces me in, closes and locks it before releasing me.

"Are you crazy?"

I look around while rubbing my neck. We're in a garage where Stefan's Bugatti is parked. There's another car under a cover, too. I've never been in here before.

"Stay here until I'm gone," he tells me, walking to a small cabinet and opening it, choosing a key.

"You're going after him! That was a trick!"

He opens the driver's side door and before he can get in, I'm around the car and opening the passenger door.

"You're not going with me. Get out."

I shake my head, close the door. "You need me. I'm your hostage. Stefan's soldiers will kill you before you make it to the property gates without me here."

"Car's bulletproof. Get out."

"They'll shoot the tires."

"We don't have time for this."

Something rams against the door and the wood splinters.

"No, we don't! Go!"

He's out of time and out of choices as the next time they ram whatever it is they've got into the door, it opens.

"Get down!" Rafa yells as he hits the gas and we crash through the garage door and out onto the dirt road.

Machine guns fire but soon stop. They must know I'm in the car, too. It gives Rafa the edge he needs to get off the property, just making it through the still open gates before they close on him, the Bugatti bouncing and screeching as he hits the main road hard and we're on our way.

34

STEFAN

I'm not one to obey commands. Catalano must know this.

The man behind me twists my arms.

I lean my head forward then ram the back of it into his nose. I don't have to turn around to see the damage. I hear it. And I felt it. I just broke his nose and he's in a world of pain. As soon as my arms are free, I slam an elbow into his gut.

Rifles are aimed at me as I straighten, adjust my jacket sleeves and glare at Catalano.

"That was a mistake, Stefan," he says as he raises his pistol inches from my face.

I grip his forearm and when he cocks the weapon, I aim it away.

"You're outnumbered. Outmaneuvered," he says.

"And you overestimate yourself."

"You've always been a cocky son of a bitch."

"I don't take kindly to people who insult my mother."

"Fuck you, Stefan. You piece of shit."

"Stefan," Lucas says.

I turn to find three men with weapons aimed at his chest and head.

Well, Catalano's right that we're outnumbered, at least for the moment, but we're nowhere near outmaneuvered.

I give Catalano a smirk and let go of his forearm.

He takes a moment, probably trying to gauge if I'm going to break his nose the minute he puts his gun down.

I'm not.

"Francesco," I say, my tone musical, my voice relaxed. Because men like him, I know. Men like him, I crush.

He uncocks his pistol and drops his arm but doesn't put the gun away. "Cuff him," he orders one of his men.

A moment later, my hands are cuffed in front of me. At least they're not behind me.

"Show me in," I say.

I follow him to a room at the end of the hall. He pushes open the doors and I take inventory.

I'm not surprised, really. Well, maybe a little.

Two uncles from Syracuse are sitting at the rectangular table. Along with them are their boys, that makes a total of six plus Catalano. Seven.

Them I expect.

It's Gabriel Marchese sitting with a smirk on his face I don't expect.

"Stefan," he says, that smirk spreading into a wide, satisfied grin as he stands, extending his hand to me. "What a surprise."

I study him, try to see any resemblance to Gabriela, and happily see none.

"Dad," I say, smiling wide myself as I take his hand, my hard grip matching his.

He loosens his grip to let me go, but I hold tight, my smile a sneer.

For one moment, Marchese's face is wiped clean of his grin.

I drop his hand, take in the other men in my periphery. Four soldiers. Catalano's men.

From the looks on their faces, it's clear no one expected to see me.

Lucas takes his place to my right.

"Gentlemen," I say.

The Syracuse men glance at one another. "S...Stefan," one begins to rise, and the others follow.

I go to the first one, extend my cuffed hand to shake his.

"Uncle. It's good to see you. And my cousins."

I look the men over. Young, this one. Eighteen, if I recall. The others are older. I make a mental note of who they are. They'll be dealt with if they survive the night.

After we've all shaken hands, I pull a chair over from across the room and set it at the table, gesture for Catalano to take the seat as I make my way to the head of the table.

Catalano's face betrays annoyance, then rage.

"I didn't realize we did business with people outside our family," I say to him.

"Business is business. This is the new way of doing things."

"So let me guess. My father-in-law is here to support you financially."

Catalano falters. He glances around the table, his expression uneasy.

Marchese clears his throat. "Hardly matters where the money comes from as long as it's there."

"Let's get on with things," I say. "You were taking a vote?"

Catalano sits. "We've already voted."

"And? I'm curious about the results."

"You don't belong at the head of this once-great family, Stefan," Catalano says.

"You're not even part of this family, Francesco," I remind him.

Hate dulls his dark eyes. "Rafa is. You can't deny that."

"Rafa is not a blood cousin to the Sabbioni."

He smirks. "No. He's more than that."

"Francesco," one of the Syracuse men warns.

Catalano doesn't take his eyes off me. "It's time he knew. Past time."

"Then do tell," I say, sounding calmer than I feel because I have a very bad feeling about this.

"You Sabbioni think you're mightier than the rest of us. Better, somehow. More entitled to life."

"I think no such thing."

"How have you ever treated Rafa?"

"Like a brother. How have you treated him?"

"Funny you say that," he starts, not bothering to answer my question. "See, there's a reason your father was so good to him."

"Because he was my aunt's son. And my father loved my aunt."

"Yes, he did. That's one thing we can agree on."

I wait.

"Very much. He loved both sisters, didn't he? Had a hard time deciding between them."

"Be careful, Francesco. Be very careful."

I see every one of his yellowing teeth when he smiles. "No need for me to be careful anymore," he says, gesturing to his armed men. "As I was saying, your father loved both sisters."

I think about what Rafa had said over and over again. That he's like a brother to me. That he *is* a brother to me.

I grow very still, understanding slowly what Catalano has. Or thinks he has.

"He's older than you by two months."

"He is."

"And that gives him the right to rule."

I wait. Because I need to hear the words.

"Your father never could keep his dick in his pants."

At that, I lunge for him, but two sets of hands close over my shoulders and push me back into my seat and as soon as Lucas moves from his place, another soldier shoves the barrel of his gun into his chest.

"But I blame your mother, really. Couldn't satisfy her husband so he had to go slithering about and my whore wife, well, she spread her legs wide for that snake."

"I'm going to kill you slow, Francesco."

He laughs outright at that and I grip the edges of the table. My guess is I have another four, five minutes tops before my men raid this place. I want to be sure Francesco survives because I want to do the killing myself.

"Here," he says, reaching into his pocket. "Proof, if you need it. Our cousins have already seen the DNA report."

"Francesco," one of the Syracuse cousins starts.

Catalano holds up his hand, eyes locked on me. "Quiet, cousin. We took the vote."

"Tell me how you each voted."

"It was unanimous," Catalano answers.

"You'll understand if I want to hear from each man's mouth."

"You should have killed Marchese when you had the chance, Stefan," one of the cousins says. "It's weakened you, this game you're playing. Weakened us."

"How exactly? I'll be taking over Marchese's ships. You have to think farther than next week, cousin."

"It's personal for you."

"Yeah, it's fucking personal. He's the reason Antonio

turned on us. He's the reason my father is dead. And he's the man who had Antonio killed."

He drops his gaze.

"Too much talking," Francesco starts, standing. "Take him out back. Kill him like the dog he is," he tells the soldiers.

It takes two of them to haul me to my feet and even then, I manage to punch one in the face and the other gets an elbow in the gut before they manage to move me.

I think about Gabriela. About what they'll do to her if they get to her.

I think about my promise to her.

My promise to come back to her.

But when they manage to shuffle me to the door, it opens in on us and Rafa stands on the other side of it, and behind him, Gabriela comes running.

Fuck!

"Get her out of here!" I order someone. Anyone.

Rafa looks back, catches her when she tries to come into the room.

"I told you to take the fucking car! To go!"

"Get off me!" She struggles against him, eyes on me, then on the men around me.

"Gabriela!" Marchese is behind me. "What's she doing here?" I'm not sure who he's asking.

"Let her go!" I shout. Fuck. This fucks things up. "Lucas. Get her out of here."

"No!" she cries.

I have one, two minutes maybe before all hell breaks loose.

"Good you're here," Catalano says, looking at Rafa. "You should be the one to do it. Kill him and take your place. Claim your birthright."

Rafa looks from me to Catalano and back.

"Let him go," Rafa commands the soldiers who have me.

"I give the orders, Rafa. Until he's dead," Catalano says.

Rafa looks to Catalano, then back to me.

"How long have you known?" I ask Rafa.

"A few months."

"Months?"

He nods.

"Why didn't you tell me yourself?"

He shrugs a shoulder, can't quite hold my gaze. When he finally forces himself to I see that same look in his eyes as I saw earlier. Sadness. Regret.

"I'm sorry, Stefan," he says.

"Get her out of here," I tell him. "She doesn't need to see this."

Rafa nods, gestures to one of Catalano's soldiers.

Lucas glances at me. He knows what's coming.

The soldier takes hold of Gabriela and drags her kicking and screaming from the room.

That's when all hell breaks loose.

When windows crash and guns blaze and smoke and screams and blood and flesh explode around us, every man ducking for cover, every man drawing a weapon and shooting blind.

I'm knocked to the floor.

"No!" someone yells but I can't tell who.

My men rush around me and everything happens in slow motion as I take a dropped pistol and get to my feet, opening fire on any Catalano man or cousin left alive and holding a weapon.

My mind is on her, my brain telling me she wouldn't have had time to get out while simultaneously trying to block the thought.

She's out. She's safe. She has to be.

Because none of this will matter if she's not.

The gunfire quiets, no more machine guns. It probably lasted all of two minutes but felt like an eternity.

As smoke clears, I take in the room, the carnage. What we leave in our wake in my family.

Collateral damage.

It's what most of them become.

It's what she was.

"Gabriela!"

I walk out of the room, count the bodies. Take in the blood.

"Gabriela!"

I see him first. Marchese on the floor, on top of her.

Blood pools around them and he's not moving. Is she?

My steps slow.

Fuck.

Fuck.

Why was she here?

Why did he bring her here?

"Stefan," it's Rafa from behind me.

I don't turn. I don't care.

I get to them. Look at the expanding pool of blood.

I drop to my knees in it.

The floor is hard, the blood warm. It seeps into my jeans and I know Rafa's calling me again but it's like an echo, a distant sound.

Dropping the pistol, I push Marchese's body off her, barely taking notice of him. Her eyes are closed and she's not moving.

"Gabriela." Even my own voice, it's strange, that echo again. Like we're in a tunnel.

She makes a sound, coughs, and her fingers move, streaking blood.

I roll her gently over, touch her, feel for a bullet wound, but the blood isn't hers.

She blinks her eyes open, touches her head. "Stefan?"

I smile. In this terrible moment, I smile, and I lift her into my arms.

Her forehead's bleeding. The impact of Marchese falling on top of her must have knocked her out.

I hold her to me with my cuffed hands, closing my eyes, kissing the top of her head, thanking God. Because it's what we do in moments like this, believers and atheists.

It's then she turns to see her father. It takes her a moment to register the fact that he's not moving.

"Dad?" She pulls away from me, touches his face. "Dad?"

I watch them. See his eyes open, but it's weak.

"Dad." Her voice breaks.

His hand moves, reaches for hers. He can barely move it.

She takes it and blood soaks her fingers.

His lips move, but I don't hear any sound. She must hear what he says though because she begins to cry softly, leaning down toward him.

His eyes close then and I hear the grief she's feeling. I hear it in her sob.

Marchese saved her life. He shielded her from the bullet that would have killed her and died in her place.

"Stefan."

I finally look up. Rafa stands beside Catalano. Catalano is holding a pistol in each hand, Rafa's bleeding from his shoulder, but Catalano is unhurt.

I leave Gabriela with her father's body and rise to my feet.

It's not over.

"Do it," Catalano says, holding a pistol out to Rafa. "Do it, or I will."

Rafa takes the gun and walks toward me and I look at my cousin, my brother, at this man I would give my life for. Will he take it now? Will he be the one to take it now?

"I'm sorry," Rafa says, coming to stand before me.

I catch him when he stumbles. He's hurt worse than I realized.

"Rafa," I start, sliding my hand over his, the one that's holding the gun.

Rafa looks over his shoulder at Catalano and I know the answer to my unasked question. And so does Catalano.

"Fucking waste of space," Catalano curses and raises his arm and just before he fires, Rafa meets my eyes and raises himself to his full height for one single, final moment.

I feel the impact of it with him. I feel him jolt, feel the breath forced from him.

And I take the gun from his hand and shoot Catalano, emptying it in him, sending him backward, drumming bullets into his stomach until the pistol clicks, empty and useless. Until there are no bullets and the only sound is that of my screaming as I drop to my knees with Rafa in my arms.

Rafa's body limp in my arms.

"Fuck. Rafa. Don't..."

"Brothers. Who knew?" he says, giving me that goofy smile one last time. One last fucking time before his eyes close.

"Rafa. No. Fuck. Don't fucking die! God, please..."

I hold him and rock with him and I think this is worse than when I found out Antonio had died. When I saw Antonio's body.

I think this is somehow sadder. Can you rate death as sad or sadder or saddest? It's wrong.

All the loss. All the fucking loss.

And for what?

His lips are open, breath shallow as his chest barely rises and falls.

Gabriela crawls to me, and I see she's crying too, pushing Rafa's bloodied hair from his face, and he looks so young. Like a kid almost. Like he used to.

I think about how sorry I am as sirens wail in the background. I think about how much I'm going to miss him.

"Hold on, brother. Hold the fuck on."

35

STEFAN

Any luck I've ever had has been bad.

But that night in the warehouse, that luck finally took a turn. Or maybe there is a God. And maybe he heard me. Because I'm sitting beside Rafa's hospital bed holding a fucking cup to his mouth as he drinks water from a straw and I'm so fucking grateful. I am so fucking grateful.

"You look like shit, you know that?" he says to me.

I set the cup aside and smile. It's been almost a week since the shooting. I haven't left the hospital since we got here so yeah, I probably look like shit.

"Pot calling the kettle black," I say. And what I feel, it's elation. All that's happened, what he did...all I can think is that he's alive. He's alive. "I'm going to beat the shit out of you when you get out of here."

A shadow crosses his features just as the door opens and we both turn to find Gabriela walk inside.

I stand, smile at her, wrap my arm around her waist. She has some scratches, some bumps, but she's fine. Again, I'm grateful.

"How do you feel?" she asks Rafa.

"Pain killers are doing their work," he says.

He was badly injured. The bullet his father put in him missed his heart by a hair or this would be much worse. That wasn't the only bullet he took but it was the worst.

She touches the bandage on his face. "Girls like scars, right?" He'll have one across his right cheek, a constant reminder of how close he came to death.

He doesn't smile. "I'm sorry," he says, looking from her to me. "I'm sorry for all of it. I knew better and I'm sorry."

My throat tightens.

Gabriela pushes hair off Rafa's face then leans down to kiss his forehead and whispers something to him. She straightens, turns to me and slides her hands into mine.

"I'll wait for you outside. You need to come home with me Stefan."

I nod, squeeze her hands. I don't watch her go.

Rafa stares up at me.

"You almost died," I say, sitting back down.

"I deserved to die. Part of me wanted to. I betrayed you, Stefan. And all you've ever been is a brother to me. Blood or not."

"You took a bullet for me. That's what I know," I pause, consider what I'm about to say. It may be the thing to seal his fate. "I do have one question for you."

The way he looks at me, it's like he knows what I'm going to ask before I ask it. Knows the importance of his answer.

"Did you know they'd put Gabriela at the bottom of that well?"

His face contorts, eyes wet as he shakes his head. "No. I didn't know they'd do that to her. Believe it or not, I never wanted her hurt."

I do believe it. Maybe it's stupid of me, but I do.

The door opens again and Gabriela peers inside. "The car's here."

I nod, stand and when Rafa's hand closes over mine, I see on his face the pain it costs him.

I close my other hand over his and I look at him and think about what he's lost too. And I know myself. I don't forgive easily. And I never forget. But I want to.

"Get better, brother."

EPILOGUE 1

STEFAN

It's been three months since everything.

For three months, I haven't let Gabriela out of my sight. For three months, I've woken in the night to look at her. To touch her. To feel her beside me. To know she's there. To know she's real.

I look at her now, too, in the glow of the moon. The night is clear but cooler than the last time we sailed out here. Out to Skull Rock.

She's quiet but she smiles more even if her smiles are sad.

I think that's always going to be a part of her. That sadness. It's woven into the fabric of her. It makes her who she is.

But it's changing little by little. Those smiles, they appear more and more.

I bring the boat up to the beach and climb out. She stands as I secure it before helping her out. We're both bare-foot and the sand feels good.

"How cold will it be here in winter?" she asks.

"Mild. Nowhere near as cold as New York."

We sit on the sand and I follow her gaze to the sky. I remember our last conversation when we were here. It was the day of Alex's memorial service and she'd told me she believed we became those stars when we died.

"Are you looking for your mom?" I ask her.

She nods. "Dad too."

I squeeze her hand. "He did the right thing in the end."

She glances at me, exhales. "A single heroic act does not a hero make, Stefan. But it must mean something."

"It does."

She turns away, and I can see she's struggling to believe that. "What happens with you and Rafa now?" she asks when she shifts her gaze back to mine.

After his release from the hospital, Rafa left. It was a mutual decision. Things can't go back to what they were. I think he and I both know that. But I also wasn't ready to do what I, as head of the family, should do.

"I don't know."

"He saved your life."

"I know. But the family has suffered again due to betrayal. I can't let that go."

"He's been punished enough, don't you think? He lost everything."

"He lost everything he would have stolen from me."

"You don't care about that more than you care about him."

She's right. And he did lose it all. Even Clara. Although I'm not sure that was such a big loss.

"What happens if I let this go? History repeats, Gabriela, unless we break the cycles."

"Then punish him if you have to but bring him back. You miss him. I see it, Stefan. I feel it."

"You're gentle. After everything." I study her face in the

moonlight. "I love you. Do you know that?" I ask. "I watch you at night, when you sleep."

"Creeper." She makes a face that makes me smile at least momentarily.

"I don't know what I would do without you."

"I don't want us to ever find that out. I love you, Stefan. I remember the first time you said that. I told you I hated you and you said I didn't. You said that I loved you. That was when I knew."

I sit up, reach into my pocket. "I have something for you." I take it out, keep it in the palm of my hand.

She sits up too. Waits.

"I want to make this right. Do it again, do it right."

"What are you talking about?"

"Give me your hand," I tell her, taking her left hand. I take both the engagement ring and the wedding band off and pocket them.

"What are you doing?"

"You didn't like those, did you?"

"No, I didn't. A little over the top."

"Hideous. Like how this started."

I open my hand and she looks at it, at the ring in the center of my palm.

"What is it?"

"What does it look like?"

She meets my eyes. "Don't be an ass."

I smile, take the ring and bring it to her finger. "This is my mother's wedding ring. My father gave it to her. It's an old Sabbioni family ring, more than a hundred years old."

"It's beautiful," she says, looking down at it.

"Will you marry me, Gabriela?"

"We're already married, Stefan."

"Now who's being an ass?"

She laughs.

"Well?"

"Ask me again?"

"Gabriela Marchese, will you marry me and be my wife and the mother of my children?"

"How many kids are we talking?"

"A dozen. To start."

"You're crazy, you know that?" she asks, her eyes bright, her smile wide.

I wait.

"Yes. Yes, I'll marry you, again, this time of my own free will, and I will have your babies and fill that house up. Fill it up with noise and laughter and happiness."

I slide the ring onto her finger and pull her to me. "I love you."

"I love you."

I draw back to kiss her and that kiss, it's as though it seals something between us. And when I lay her down and strip off her clothes and make love to her, I never once let her go. I hold her and I fill her up and I know this is it. I know that for me, *she* is it.

This woman, this pawn that I took from my enemy is mine. And ironically, we saved each other.

EPILOGUE 2

GABRIELA

Six Months Later

The sky burns orange behind me. I'm wearing my mother's dress. It was her mother's before her and her mother's before that.

The breeze blows from the sea, salty and cool, the sunset one of the most beautiful I've seen since coming to Italy. A gift, maybe.

"Are you ready?" Gabe asks me.

I turn to him, look up into his handsome, sweet face. I don't think about what could have been for him. I can't do that anymore. He is here. He is alive. And I think he's happy. Maybe he's happier than he would have been if none of this had happened.

"You look really handsome in your suit, Gabe," I say, adjusting his tie.

"Thanks, Gabi. You're so beautiful. You look like mom. You make me remember her face."

Tears warm my eyes.

"I think she's watching us sometimes," he says.

"Me too. I know she is."

He smiles.

I think about all that's happened. All the things I know. The things I don't want to know. Like what Stefan had on my father that made him give me up in the first place. I don't want to know that. I know it will be terrible and what I know about him is terrible enough.

I think, instead, about what he did. His final act on earth.

He saved my life.

He died to save me.

When I told Gabe, he cried. But then he said something unexpected and so wise. He said he was happy dad was at peace. I love that about him. I love Gabe's innocence.

The old door of the chapel creaks and someone peers their head out. It's Miss Millie.

"Ready?" she whispers.

I nod.

Gabe lifts the veil to lay it over my head, covering my face. Yellowed lace obscures my vision as I turn to the chapel, look at the old stone walls, at the tall, arched stained glass windows depicting scenes from the Bible.

When Gabe takes my arm and tucks it into his, the doors open and organ music trickles out, the opening notes of the piece Stefan chose. We step onto the carpet and Gabe squeezes my arm when the few people gathered stand and turn to us.

I breathe in the scent of incense, remembering Alex. Knowing he's watching over us too.

I only glimpse Miss Millie's face for a moment before the soprano begins her song, the music rising, and my gaze falls on Stefan standing at the end of the aisle. He stands alone and I think Rafa should be here. Rafa should be by his side.

I hope one day he can be.

But I can't think about that now. Past is past. Today is the beginning of our future.

Stefan smiles as I walk toward him and I feel Gabe's grip tighten, feel that tender, reassuring squeeze again. Stefan looks as handsome as ever, even as the hair at his temple has greyed a little, even as there's one more crease on his forehead.

When we reach the altar, the priest speaks.

"Who gives this woman to marry this man?" he asks.

"I do," Gabe says.

The priest nods, and I turn to my brother. He lifts my veil and leans down to kiss my cheek. "Don't cry," he whispers.

I respond with a loud sniffle and hug my brother. He hands me to Stefan and takes his place at my side.

Stefan smiles, squeezes my hands and kisses my cheek. "You're so beautiful."

"So are you," I say.

"And now you'll stop crying. No more tears. Understand?" he asks, pulling back.

I nod and we turn to the priest and all I can think throughout the ceremony, as we listen to the mass, as we take our vows and exchange our rings, all I can think is how happy I am. How right this is.

How I belong here.

How I belong with Stefan and Stefan belongs with me.

And when the priest gives us his blessing and instructs Stefan to kiss his bride, I think this is it. This is my wedding day, even if on paper it's months ago that we were married.

I remember saying to Rafa how it wasn't the real deal when he congratulated me then. Well, this is the real deal.

And there's nothing I want more.

Well, maybe a dozen of Stefan's babies.

The End

THANK YOU

Thank you for reading *The Collateral Damage Duet*. I hope you enjoyed it and would consider leaving a review.

If you loved Collateral Damage, you may enjoy The Dark Legacy Trilogy. Keep reading for a sample from *Taken*!

If you'd like to keep updated on dates and news, please sign up for my newsletter and consider joining my Facebook Group, The Knight Spot.

TAKEN SAMPLE

PROLOGUE

Helena

I'm the oldest of the Willow quadruplets. Four girls. Always girls. Every single quadruplet birth, generation after generation, it's always girls.

This generation's crop yielded the usual, but instead of four perfect, beautiful dolls, there were three.

And me.

And today, our twenty-first birthday, is the day of harvesting.

That's the Scafoni family's choice of words, not ours. At least not mine. My parents seem much more comfortable with it than my sisters and I do, though.

Harvesting is always on the twenty-first birthday of the quads. I don't know if it's written in stone somewhere or what, but it's what I know and what has been on the back of my mind since I learned our history five years ago.

There's an expression: *those who cannot remember the past are condemned to repeat it.* Well, that's bullshit, because we Willows know well our past and yet, here we are. The same blocks that have been used for centuries standing in the old library, their surfaces softened by the feet of every other Willow Girl who stood on the same stumps of wood, and all I can think when I see them, the four lined up like they are, is how archaic this is, how fucking unreal. How they can't do this to us.

Yet, here we are.

And they are doing this to us.

But it's not *us*, really.

My shift is marked.

I'm *unclean*.

So it's really my sisters.

Sometimes I'm not sure who I hate more, my own family for allowing this insanity generation after generation, or the Scafoni monsters for demanding the sacrifice.

"It's time," my father says. His voice is grave.

He's aged these last few months. I wonder if that's remorse because it certainly isn't backbone. I heard he and my mother argue once, exactly once, and then it was over. He simply accepted it. Accepted that tonight, his daughters will be made to stand on those horrible blocks while a Scafoni bastard looks us over, prods and pokes us, maybe checks our teeth like you would a horse, before making his choice. Before taking one of my sisters as his for the next three years of her life.

I'm not naive enough to be unsure what that will mean exactly. Maybe my sisters are, but not me.

"Up on the block. Now, Helena."

I look at my sisters who already stand so meekly on their appointed stumps. They're all paler than usual tonight and I swear I can hear their hearts pounding in fear of what's to come.

When I don't move right away, my father painfully takes

my arm and lifts me up onto my block and all I can think, the one thing that gives me the slightest hope, is that if Sebastian Scafoni chooses me, I will find some way to end this. I won't condemn my daughters to this fate. My nieces. My granddaughters.

But he won't choose me, and I think that's why my parents are angrier than usual with me.

See, I'm the ugly duckling. At least I'd be considered ugly standing next to my sisters.

And the fact that I'm unclean—not a virgin—means I won't be taken.

The Scafoni bastard will choose one of their precious golden daughters instead.

Golden, to my dark. Golden—quite literally. Sparkling almost, my sisters.

I glance at them as my father attaches the iron shackle to my ankle. He doesn't do this to any of them. They'll do as they're told, even as their gazes bounce from the closed twelve-foot doors to me and back again and again and again.

But I have no protection to offer. Not tonight. Not on this one.

The backs of my eyes burn with tears I refuse to shed.

"How can you do this? How can you allow it?" I ask for the hundredth time. I'm talking to my mother while my father clasps the restraints on my wrists, making sure I won't attack the monsters.

"Better gag her, too."

It's my mother's response to my question and, a moment later, my father does as he's told and ensures my silence.

I hate my mother more, I think. She's a Willow quadruplet. She witnessed a harvesting herself. Witnessed the result of this cruel tradition.

Tradition.

A tradition of kidnapping.

Of breaking.

Of destroying.

I look to my sisters again. Three almost carbon copies of each other, with long blonde hair curling around their shoulders, flowing down their backs, their blue eyes wide with fear. Well, except in Julia's case. She's different than the others. She's more...eager. But I don't think she has a clue what they'll do to her.

Me, no one would guess I came from the same batch.

Opposite their gold, my hair is so dark a black, it appears almost blue, with one single, wide streak of silver to relieve the stark shade, a flaw I was born with. And contrasting their cornflower-blue eyes, mine are a midnight sky; there too, the only relief the silver specks that dot them.

They look like my mother. Like perfect dolls.

I look like my great-aunt, also named Helena, down to the silver streak I refuse to dye. She's in her nineties now. I wonder if they had to lock her in her room and steal her wheelchair, so she wouldn't interfere in the ceremony.

Aunt Helena was the chosen girl of her generation. She knows what's in store for us better than anyone.

"They're coming," my mother says.

She has super hearing, I swear, but then, a moment later, I hear them too.

A door slams beyond the library, and the draft blows out a dozen of the thousand candles that light the huge room.

A maid rushes to relight them. No electricity. Tradition, I guess.

If I were Sebastian Scafoni, I'd want to get a good look at the prize I'd be fucking for the next year. And I have no doubt there will be fucking, because what else can break a girl so completely but taking that of all things?

And it's not just the one year. No. We're given for three years. One year for each brother. Oldest to youngest. It used to be four, but now, it's three.

I would pinch my arm to be sure I'm really standing here, that I'm not dreaming, but my hands are bound behind my back, and I can't.

This can't be fucking real. It can't be legal.

And yet here we are, the four of us, naked beneath our translucent, rotting sheaths—I swear I smell the decay on them—standing on our designated blocks, teetering on them. I guess the Willows of the past had smaller feet. And I admit, as I hear their heavy, confident footfalls approaching the ancient wooden doors of the library, I am afraid.

I'm fucking terrified.

Available in all stores!

ALSO BY NATASHA KNIGHT

Collateral Damage Duet

Collateral: an Arranged Marriage Mafia Romance

Damage: an Arranged Marriage Mafia Romance

Dark Legacy Trilogy

Taken (Dark Legacy, Book 1)

Torn (Dark Legacy, Book 2)

Twisted (Dark Legacy, Book 3)

MacLeod Brothers

Devil's Bargain

Benedetti Mafia World

Salvatore: a Dark Mafia Romance

Dominic: a Dark Mafia Romance

Sergio: a Dark Mafia Romance

The Benedetti Brothers Box Set (Contains Salvatore, Dominic and Sergio)

Killian: a Dark Mafia Romance

Giovanni: a Dark Mafia Romance

The Amado Brothers

Dishonorable

ACKNOWLEDGMENTS

Cover Design by Jay Aheer, Simply Defined Art

Editing by Casey McKay

Sketch by Manuela Soriani

ABOUT THE AUTHOR

USA Today bestselling author of contemporary romance, Natasha Knight specializes in dark, tortured heroes. Happily-Ever-Afters are guaranteed, but she likes to put her characters through hell to get them there. She's evil like that.

Want more?
www.natasha-knight.com
natasha-knight@outlook.com